HEARTLESS

MERCILESS BOOK 2

W WINTERS

AUTHOR'S COPYRIGHT

PROLOGUE

Carter

Rain is coming. The kind of rain that makes your bones ache. The dark gray sky is streaked with dry lightning that splinters the crack of pain even deeper.

There's only so much a man can take. Only so far he can be pushed to the brink and still want to survive.

First, my mother lost her fight with cancer.

Then Tyler, my youngest brother, was struck and killed by a car.

And now, my father has been murdered in cold blood.

The blame for my father's death is easy to place. A group of thugs who wanted the highest high, and they were willing to do whatever it took to chase it.

They didn't fear my father. Not like they fear me.

I know that's why they waited for him to be the one on the street corner, instead of me dealing from the back of the truck. When my mother died, selling drugs was what we needed to do to pay the bills. But months have passed, and it's more than an income stream now. Dealing, and the fighting that comes with, it is now my obsession.

I'm not just peddling dope or selling off stolen prescriptions. The drug trade is lucrative beyond anything I could have ever dreamed.

But Talvery taught me more than anyone else could.

He taught me where the boundaries were. Taught me what fear is capable of.

He showed me what it takes to make the pain go away and replace it with something more addictive than heroin. Power is everything.

And I feel it flowing through my veins.

Crack! Lightning strikes again, followed by a boom and shaking of the ground.

Rain is coming, but I'll stand here for as long as it takes.

The priest's voice is a dull monotone and the cries from distant family members, who I've only ever seen a handful of times in my life, numb me.

The casket in which my father's body lies reflects the first droplets of water. The sprinkling is just the beginning of the downpour threatening to fall any minute now.

He would still be alive if they'd had the same fear of him that they have of me. If he'd learned the hard lesson Talvery had taught me months ago.

Revenge will come for the pricks who killed my father. Not because I love him. Or *loved*, rather. I think I hated him in the last few years. Truly and deeply despised the piece of shit he became when my mother got sick. The realization is freeing.

That's not why I'll hunt down each and every one of those assholes and take a baseball bat to them in their sleep, or a gun to the side of their heads as they creep through dark back alleys, or a knife along their throats in the restrooms of their favorite bars. One by one, I'll kill them all.

It's not because I want revenge or because I don't want my father's death to go unanswered.

No. I'll murder them because they thought they could take from me. They decided it was worth the risk to take from me. Anger rises in my chest, heating my blood and forcing my hands into white-knuckled fists. I have to clench my teeth in an effort to hide the rage.

No one will ever take from me again. They won't take more of my family. They won't take a goddamn thing from me. Never again.

THE DAY my father was laid to rest, the demon who had long slept inside of me awakened and destroyed whatever bit of goodness that had lingered in my heart. From that day forward, I decided that everyone would fear me. Simply because it was easier to survive that way, obsessing over the power that fear would bring me.

I craved their fear the way I used to pray for the pain to go away.

It was all-consuming and only the tiniest slivers of this new armor ever broke off. Only when painful memories forced me to confront who and what I used to be. But even the smallest shards of my armor were so easily replaced by the blood of those who dared to threaten what I'd become.

So long as everyone feared me and those closest to me, I would not only survive, I would thrive.

They needed to fear my brothers.

And now they need to fear her. *My songbird.*

They will. I refuse to let anyone take her.

No one will take her away from me. No one.

CHAPTER 1

Aria

I CAN'T STOP SHAKING. My entire body is consumed by fear and I'm trembling all over. My hands are shaking chaotically, and I can't make them stop.

The heavy knife is gripped tighter than I've ever gripped anything in my life. I don't even feel like it's my hand holding the weapon. Another person's hand, on top of mine, is forcing it to stay in my grip. To hold it tighter and tighter until it hurts so much that my body begs me to fall to my knees in agony.

I won't allow my body to betray me. I can't drop the knife. I can't stop myself. The fear and rage are mingling into a concoction that's far too powerful to deny.

The blood on the blade drips down onto my hand

and feels like fire on my skin. The tension, the anger, the pure rage, and terror all boil in my blood as I stare at the dead, milky white eyes of the monster in front of me.

I can't look at Carter. I can't rip my gaze from the motionless stare of Alexander Stephan.

I'm waiting for him to blink. To jump up and grab me. The fear I feel is paralyzing, but the adrenaline coursing through me is going to burst my veins. He's limp in the chair, his throat split wide open although the blood isn't gushing anymore. It's only a slow trickle at this point.

It reminds me of the way my mother's throat was slit. *The way he did it.*

I remember it so clearly. That scene has haunted my dreams for as long as I can remember. How he stood behind her after he'd abused her. How he didn't do it slowly; instead it was vicious and violent. It was all I could think to do to him here in this chair and at my mercy when Carter handed me the knife.

"Aria," Carter's voice breaks through my terror and the memory as he commands, "Give. Me. The. Knife." His words mix with the sound of my heavy breathing.

Carter's voice is demanding and on the edge of anger. I barely peek at him, the fear of Stephan waking and taking the knife from me is all too real. Blood seeps into his shirt, and his mangled body is unmoving. But I know he's going to take the knife back. Stephan will take it and do to me what he did to my mother.

I squeeze the steel handle harder. I won't let him.

Tears prick my eyes as Carter yells at me, his

voice booming in the silent room and sending a violent vibration through my chest. It hurts. It all hurts.

My head shakes in defiance. I shouldn't disobey him. Bad things happen when I do. *The cell.* At the thought, my shoulders hunch and my knees go weak, ready to surrender and kneel to the man who's held me captive yet given me this revenge.

Given me the means to avenge my mother's death.

But I can't move. "I can't," I say, and my words are weak and fall from my lips like a pathetic whimper. "I won't." Those two words come out harder and I reach out, swinging my arm violently in the air and slicing into Stephan's throat again. In my periphery, I see a man back away, and then another.

A small cry slips through my lips unbidden as Carter wraps his hand around mine, his other hand on my shoulder and keeping me steady as he pries my fingers back. The murmurs of the other men in the room barely register. All I can hear is Carter shushing me, and all I can focus on are Stephan's eyes. The depths of his irises never seemed as dark as they do now.

The steady shaking of my shoulders turns violent as I try to move backward, away from the monster, away from his grasp. To run and hide like I did all those years ago.

But I can't. Carter won't let me.

It's Carter, I tell myself. Carter is holding me. Focusing on regulating my shaky breathing helps steady me back to reality.

My left knee falls to the ground first and it makes my right knee slam against the ground.

"Shh," Carter shows me mercy. Stealing the knife from me but guarding me against my fears.

"It's over," he whispers as he finally pries the knife from my grasp. And I let him. I let him take it, but I won't move until I know Stephan is dead.

"He'll come for me," the scared child inside of me speaks. He can't be dead, because then it would be over. And with Stephan, it's never over. He's haunted me for as long as I can remember.

"She's fucking insane." The sharp and disgusted voice of Romano cuts through my thoughts. *Thump, thump.* My heart beats harder as I remember where I am. "This is insane," Romano says with anger.

"Shut up." Carter's voice once again tears through my body, thrumming through my blood and for the first time, I close my eyes. But then I remember Stephan is only feet from me, and they fly open again.

The room falls silent, just as Carter commanded. His fingertips are gentle on my shoulders, one hand on each as he lowers his lips to my ear and tells me, "Go upstairs and wash yourself off."

My head shakes on its own, my eyes not moving from the body in the chair in front of me.

"He's not dead," I speak softly as if it's my excuse. Logically, I know he's dead. He must be. But the fear that he's not is so real, so visceral that I can't contain it. I can't shut it down.

Carter's grip on me tightens as I hear him breathe heavier before huffing a low sound mixed with a grunt of anger. The second he moves away from me, all I feel is the chill of loneliness.

With one heavy step, Carter kicks over the chair, sending Stephan's heavy body to the floor with a thud, and again the men back up while Romano says something I can't hear. It all turns to white noise as Carter kicks the limp body. Stephan's head falls to the side and I have to move to my right, my knees rubbing against the unforgiving floor as I look into his eyes. Still open, still staring aimlessly.

"He's dead, Aria. He's fucking dead!"

My head shakes as my pulse quickens, the palms of my hands sweaty. "He can't be," I say but my words are weak.

Carter leans over the dead body, gripping my chin in both of his hands and pulling me closer to him, but I react quickly, terrified that Stephan could reach up. That he would get me if I dared to take my eyes from his.

"Un-fucking-believable." Carter's mutter sends hatred through me. Hatred toward myself and my cowardice. How many years have I woken in sheer horror at the vision of the man lying dead at my feet? Enough that logic betrays me, making me think there's no way that he's dead.

"I'll give you his head," Carter says and not understanding, my eyes lift to his for only a moment, but he's already crouching down, the knife in his hand. He lifts it high in the air and strikes it against the open wound in Stephan's throat. His muscles tense in his neck as he hardens his jaw. Anger is evident in his strained expression as he strikes again and again, taking his frustration out on Stephan's neck.

He holds the knife in place, sweating and panting with both anger and exertion. Carter's shoe slams against the slick side of the knife. Over and over each thrust of his leg is accompanied with more power, more anger—no, outrage, that Stephan's neck doesn't split beneath the blade. My body jolts with each impact, and the awe of watching Carter destroy Stephan by tearing his head from his body slowly helps restore my sanity.

A crunch that makes my gut twist and turn echoes through the room, as does the deep growl of irritation that rumbles from Carter in a snarl. As Carter lifts his bloodstained shoe, Stephan's head rolls backward, parted from his body.

My erratic heartbeat settles as Carter stands tall in front of me. His usually impeccable suit is a wrinkled mess against his tanned skin. He drops the jacket to the floor and rolls up his sleeves one by one, taking his time as he steadies his breathing. I watch every bit of him morph back into the controlled man I know him to be. With blood splattered on his shirt, his hard jawline seeming even harder in the light from the chandeliers above us, Carter has never looked more dominating as he towers over me.

Men talk around us, but they don't exist in this moment. Not when Carter's dark eyes pierce through mine and the shards of silver in them hold me hostage.

"Upstairs." The word slips from my lips before he opens his mouth. I watch as his tongue wets his lower lip and he considers me. His eyes leave mine to trail down my body and then back up, and it's only then I remind myself to breathe. "Upstairs to wash myself," I repeat Carter's command from a moment ago, letting my gaze move to Stephan's beheaded body.

When I raise my eyes back to Carter's, I know he was waiting for me to look back up at him.

I've left him waiting.

I've disobeyed him.

Everything moves around me slowly as I regain what little composure I have left.

Carter steps over Stephan's dead body and grips my chin forcefully in his hand. I can't breathe as he lowers his lips to mine, his eyes never leaving mine and tells me calmly with a voice loud enough for everyone to hear, "He'll never have power over you again. The only thing you have to fear, is me."

CHAPTER 2

Carter

"WHAT THE FUCK IS THIS, CROSS?" Romano feigns anger in his voice, but the terror is unmistakable.

Picking up Stephan's untouched and still neatly folded cloth napkin from the table, I wipe the blood from my hands and arms.

My shoulders rise and fall as I go over the last ten minutes. So little time for so much to happen. Romano isn't meant to die tonight, but I lost my composure. If he doesn't pull his shit together over Stephan dying, I'll have no choice but to kill him.

Or, if I think he'll speak a word that could ruin everything I've built and everything I have planned.

I can't hide what she does to me. I can't disguise the power Aria has over me when she doesn't listen.

Romano knows too much.

The thought forces my neck to tilt to the side and crack. And then to the other side as Romano asks again, "You set me up?"

The indignation in his voice is sickening. As if I owe him any loyalty. Dropping the napkin to the floor, I walk toward Romano, my shoes crushing fallen glass underfoot as I near him.

"He's a traitor," I say simply. "He *was* a traitor." Romano swallows and his hands ball into fists and then loosen. His gaze shifts to each person in the room. All of them with me, and none of them with him.

I could so easily destroy him. Take him out and be done with him. And then I wouldn't have to worry about the impression I've left him with. I wouldn't have to worry about him telling anyone else what Aria means to me.

But at that very thought, I know I'll let him live and walk out of my home unscathed. *I want them all to know.*

My eyes close at the realization. As I take a deep breath and fall into the calmness of my decision, I hear Jase's voice cut through the fog.

"We received some information from our leak at the Talvery headquarters," Jase says and then adds, "Stephan couldn't be trusted." His voice is calm. Calmer than Romano's as he replies with some sort of defense. I can't focus on what he says; all I can do is replay each moment in my mind, trying to decipher how Romano viewed it. How my brothers saw me. How the men who work for me watched me lose control.

They'll all know what she means to me. What she

can do to me. I want every one of those pricks to know.

As my eyes slowly open, I see Romano and I grin at him, a slow methodical grin.

"Relax, Romano," I tell him as I reach out and grip his right shoulder. I give his shoulder a firm squeeze.

I listen to his breathing hitch and watch as his pupils dilate. I've seen this look so many times before. The look of fear and hope mixing in the eyes of my enemies is undeniably familiar to me.

"He had to be dealt with, and I know you had a soft spot for him," I tell him evenly, giving his shoulder another slight squeeze as I force a faint, but kind smile to my lips. "I didn't want anyone to think you had a hand in this." I release him and add, "I know you two were close."

With my back to him, I survey the room, and a few of my men are cleaning up the evidence already. This isn't the first time blood has been shed in this room and they're more than capable of making it go away. The glass clinks as it's swept up.

"I don't have any room for traitors in my alliances," I speak to Romano, although I still have my back to him.

"I could have been informed," he responds, and I finally turn to him again.

"I thought you would enjoy the show. I was told you have a fondness for theatrics." A flash of fear sparks in his eyes and I have to school my expression to keep the sheer delight from showing. The only thing that makes this moment better is knowing that Aria is upstairs, and she'll be waiting for me.

"Next time, I'll be sure to tell you in advance." With my final words, I nod to Jase.

"I'll show you out," Jase says to Romano with a smirk and heads to the door, not waiting for his response. I merely stare at the old man and his ill-fitting suit that's rumpled and marred by a small splatter of red up his arm. His eyes narrow and his chest rises once with a heavy breath. I can only imagine the taste of blood in his mouth as he bites his tongue.

"Next time," are his parting words and they're followed by the hollow sound of his footsteps as he leaves the room.

"You want to keep any of him, boss?" Sammy asks. He's a young kid, but smart and eager to learn. Crouched near Stephan's body, he gestures to the head. "Or trash it all?" He looks up at me without any fear, but in its place is respect. I think that's why I like the kid. A very large part of me envies him. He never went through the shit I did. He didn't have to learn the way I did.

"Burn all of him. No trace. I don't want a single piece of that prick left in here."

Sammy nods once and immediately gets to work.

"How long until he turns on us?" I hear Jase's question from behind me and I turn to face my brother.

"He'd already turned on us, remember?" I remind him and Jase only smirks at me.

"He was still willing to deal with us while ripping us off. But I imagine that's going to change now." He leans against the wall and slips his hands in his pockets as he watches the men clean up the room.

"Both Talvery and Romano will come for us. You know that, right?" Daniel asks as he moves to join us. Declan follows and the four of us form a circle in the corner of the room.

"As long as they don't join forces, it doesn't matter," I respond without thinking. My thoughts immediately go back to Aria. Consequences be damned; this was for her.

"What's to stop them from doing that?" Declan asks. He wasn't concerned before tonight. Of all four of us, he's the least interested and the least informed. Because of that, I imagine he was the most shocked as well.

"A decade-long feud, greed, arrogance?" Jase answers.

"All of this, and for what?" Daniel's question comes out harder. "It was for her, wasn't it?"

Silence engulfs us for a moment as I watch my brother.

"There was no reason to go about it like this. To make a scene and piss off Romano like that."

"It had to be done." Jase is quick to answer and firm with his response.

"But we didn't have to make Romano an enemy. Not now, not when Talvery is coming for us." Daniel's anger is evident, but more so, he's scared. Scared because Addison is here with us.

"She's safe," I tell him, moving to the heart of his concern.

My brothers are quiet as I take in Daniel's stance. He's tired and anxious. "I want this shit to end, but now we've added gasoline to the fucking fire."

Jase answers before I can. I'm struck by the fact that I never considered Addison. I didn't care what the cost was for giving Aria the revenge she so desperately needed. "The guns are in, we just have to spread them and hit them hard."

"Who are we hitting? Talvery? Or Romano?" Daniel asks Jase, but then all three of my brothers look at me. All of them wanting to know.

Daniel doesn't hold back his concern as he says, "I know you've been lying to us. And now you brought war to *our* doorstep for her."

"I never lied," I mutter, and my words are a harsh whisper. Anger seeps into my blood as I watch the chaos in Daniel's eyes heat.

"What does she mean to you?" he asks as if my answer will assuage all of his fears.

Only if I answer truthfully.

Jase's gaze moves to the men behind us and then back to me with a subtle unasked question and I nod my head.

"Leave us," I call out and wait to speak until the sounds of men shuffling out of the room subside. My brothers are patient. Not speaking and holding back until we're left alone.

"She's getting to you," Daniel speaks softly. "You're making calls for all of us, but she's clouding your judgment."

His words feel like a knife in my back.

"You're questioning me?" I ask him, not holding back the bite of anger, but deep inside I know it's for me. I'm angry because he's right. My brow pinches and

I force in a deep breath and then another, staring behind my brother at the soft gray wall where bright red blood is smeared.

"She saved my life," I tell them while turning to look away. Guilt washes through me. I know I was thinking of her, not of us. But this was meant to happen. I can feel it ringing inside of me like a singular truth never has. "And I hated her for it." The confession comes out with a gentleness and careful touch.

The silence from my brothers begs me to look at them. To know for certain their reaction to my confession. Although there's a hint of shock in Daniel's eyes, there's something else there too. Something I can't place.

"Why didn't you tell us?" Jase asks. "She saved you?" he adds for clarification.

"It was years ago, the night Dad had to call his friend in." I know they know what I mean by the reference. There was only one night Dad called in a favor for me. One night where I almost met death.

"Shit," Declan bites out and runs his hand down his face. He was only a child. It was so long ago.

"As long as I'm living and breathing – she will be mine." My response is brutal and unmoving. "Whether she likes it or not."

"You took her because you hated her for saving you?" Daniel asks although there's no confrontation in his tone, nothing but genuine curiosity and concern.

"I wanted her to know what it was like to wish you could just die and not have to live another day with the person you've become." I almost tell him I didn't know that I loved her. But I change the words as I add, "I didn't know that I cared for her. Not until she came here."

She gave me a new reason to live. Not only all those years ago when she saved me, but also this past month when I finally got her beneath me.

The silence stretches between us and it feels suffocating. I've never felt shame for what I've become, because everything I am and everything I've done is for the three men who stand in front of me, judging what I've told them.

"And Stephan?" Declan asks. He's the only one of the three who didn't know why I was letting Aria kill him. He didn't care to know, like so many other things he'd rather not be aware of.

"He raped and murdered her mother. She cries at night in her sleep because of him."

The dark pit of sadness that narrowly exists within me expands at the memory of the first night I realized the power he had over her. "I had to give her this," I explain and my last word hisses from my lips.

Jase is the first to nod in agreement, followed by Declan and then, finally, Daniel.

"They're all going to be coming for us now," Daniel says, but this time his voice welcomes the challenge. The moment of wondering what my brothers think of me, what they think of *her*, ends as quickly as it came.

I answer Daniel the only way I know how. With the only acceptable answer there is.

"Let them come."

CHAPTER 3

Aria

I DON'T KNOW how long I've been shaking. My hand trembles as I reach for the faucet and turn the scalding water even hotter. My skin is bright red, but I can't feel anything. Everything is numb and out of my control as I lean against the tiled wall. My knees quiver and my body begs me to heave. The heavy diamond on the necklace ever present around my neck hits the tile of the stall and I hold on to it as if it can save me or take me away.

Is this what it feels like to kill someone? I've only seen two people die in front of me before.

My mother was the first. And the second ruled my life until the fateful day Carter changed my life forever.

I remember thinking about that second time when I

watched someone's life being taken in front of me, right as I stood at the side of the bar. Completely unaware that when I entered, my entire life would change forever. I just wanted my notebook back.

I suck in a deep breath of the hot steam as I lean my head back against the tile and close my eyes. The memory takes me back to only weeks ago, but that memory is far better than the reality of my blood-stained skin.

SHOVING *my hands in my pockets to keep them warm, I let my fingers trace over the keys to my car. It's the only weapon I have.*

And keys are a weapon. I've seen someone slice a hole in a guy's throat with a key. I stood there numbly as the man's hands tried to reach his neck, but my father's men gripped his wrists and pulled them behind his back. Blow after blow, each one puncturing his skin as he was restrained and unable to defend himself.

A chill flows over my skin at the memory and it takes me a minute to realize I'm not breathing.

I remember the sound of sneakers kicking small rocks across the pavement. The sound of the busy street at the other end of the alley.

Three men my father employs were supposed to be escorting me back home from the studio I wanted to rent, but they decided to take a detour.

And I stood there in shock; it all happened so quickly.

Mika was with me then. His thin lips tipped up into the evilest smile I'd ever seen. That smile held pure joy. Joy at my shock? Or my horror? Maybe my pain, because I knew the man they'd killed.

Mika's dark black hair was slicked back. His beard was shaved off and it was only stubble that caressed his skin that night. Conventionally speaking, Mika's a good-looking man with a deep, rough voice that can bring any woman to her knees.

But I've seen who he really is. And knowing he's the man I've come to see and make demands of, sends a spike of fear through me.

But I won't let anyone steal from me. I can't let them push me around and let them think I'm weak. And like my father says, it's time for me to demand respect. It's what the Talverys do.

MY EYES slowly open to the sound of the water hitting the bare tile. Every movement, every noise, makes my body tense.

I try to steady my breathing, ragged from the memories. The one of the night I was taken, and the other of that night two years ago when I saw a man murdered. I didn't leave home for a long time after that, and I never moved out. My father wanted it that way anyway.

I thought I knew what fear was before I walked into that bar. I was wrong.

Staring at the lifeless corpse of a man whose exis-tence has tormented you for years is true fear. It wasn't until his head rolled away from his body on the carpet, that I could even consider the possibility that he would never hurt me again.

My gaze drifts to the pool of water at my feet. The water contains dark red splotches until it swirls and morphs to pink as it flows to the drain.

First, I watched my mother's death.

Then the death of a man who betrayed my father.

And now I've killed the man who betrayed both of my parents.

I wait for a sense of relief, or victory—right-eousness, maybe. But nothing comes. There's only a hollow emptiness in my chest and a flood of unwanted memories.

The sound of the glass door to the shower sliding open nearly tears a scream from my throat.

Mika, my father, Stephan... of all the men responsible for me leading a life riddled with fear, none of them compare to the man standing in front of me. The steam billows around him as it exits the shower stall, allowing the chill of the cooler air to leave goosebumps along my skin.

Carter's gaze narrows as he assesses me, glued to the wall and still shaking, still struggling to do anything. I've never felt so weak in my life as I do right now.

Killing Stephan may have felt freeing during the moments the knife sliced into him, but I've never been so chained to memories as I am in this instant.

"What are you doing?" His deep voice comes out a question, but I don't think he expects me to answer.

"I can't stop shaking," I tell him in a staccato cadence that reflects my inability to do anything clearly. Each word is forced out as I grip my wrist with my other hand and will it to stop, finally letting go of the gem.

Carter doesn't answer me. Instead, he steps into the stall, still clothed. He hisses through his teeth as the hot water batters his arm and splashes along his blood-stained shirt, now sticking to his skin. He turns the faucet, cooling the water until it's only warm and no longer scalding hot.

The cool air feels refreshing as it caresses my skin more and more the longer he stands in front of me with the door open. My head feels light and the panic that was all-consuming only a moment ago, wanes.

In one breath, Carter strips from his shirt. In another, he closes the door behind him and pulls me into his arms. The warm water gently splashes along my back in time with Carter's soothing strokes. It takes a moment for me to return the embrace, to wrap my arms around him and press my cheek to his bare chest.

His heartbeat is steady as he holds me and it's calming. *So calming.* The trembling subsides quicker than I could imagine.

My eyes close and I welcome the darkness of exhaustion until Carter clears his throat, startling me from the comfortable silence.

"I'm sorry for telling you that I wouldn't be with you," he says and his voice rumbles up his chest. I stay tense against him, caught off guard. I barely remember his words from earlier. Everything happened so quickly; of everything that happened tonight, the last thing on my mind is the threat he gave me before I knew his intentions and every piece of the puzzle fell into place.

An apology is something I would never expect from him.

Carter is never sorry. Carter is unapologetic in everything he does.

Without an answer from me, he continues, "I shouldn't have said that. And I'm sorry for it." Another moment passes, and the cloudy haze slowly dissipates until I can peel myself away from him. My nakedness and the reality of what I am to him are slowly coming back to me.

Today has been a whirlwind of emotions. The most prevalent being pain.

I swallow thickly before stepping away from him and out of the flowing streams of water to tell him it's okay.

I don't know what else to say.

Pushing the wet hair from my face, I look him in the eyes and the intensity in his gaze sets my body on fire.

"It's not okay. And it won't happen again," Carter replies as his eyes darken and he moves in the suddenly small shower, stalking toward me to place both of his palms against the tile wall on either side of my head.

His broad shoulders eclipse everything else as he towers over me, and the sheer power that radiates from him forces a deep urge of need down to my core. The pulse is uncontrollable and threatens to overcome my senses.

It would be so easy to fall into his arms. To get lost in the lusty haze that is Carter Cross.

"I forgive you," I tell him in a single breath and try to swallow down the desire. Suddenly, I'm hotter than I was before. All over, and all at once.

My nipples pebble and my fingers itch to reach out to him, to spear my fingers through his hair and pull his lips down to mine.

But Carter doesn't kiss me. He never has. My gaze stays pinned to his lips as he lowers them, oh, so slowly, but they pass my own and travel to my shoulder. His rough stubble grazes my neck and makes my pussy throb. His tongue sweeps along my skin and a heat flows through me that I can't deny.

If I could hold on to this moment and hide from the pain of my reality forever, I would.

Just as I dare to reach up, to let my fingers travel along his shoulders and then higher, a sudden knock at the door cuts sharply through the moment.

The white noise of the shower dims as Jase's voice carries through the door, calling out to take Carter away from me.

Don't go, my heart begs me to plead with him. I can't be alone right now. *I'm not okay.*

Carter nudges the tip of his nose against mine, letting a soft hum of approval vibrate up his chest before telling Jase that he's coming. He lowers his voice and looks me in the eyes as he tells me, "Finish here and wait in bed for me."

The command and heat in his eyes is something I could never refute. "Yes, Carter," I answer obediently, and it only makes the heat between my thighs grow hotter.

It's not until he's gone that I realize how much I want him.

How much I need Carter Cross right now. I have no one else.

And how much that very fact scares me.

CHAPTER 4

Carter

"He said he's cooled off, but the fucker's already talking." Jase updates me the second I step into the den. The adrenaline from tonight had subsided. The ringing in my blood had dulled.

Until I saw Aria still shaking.

One look at her delicate form trembling from the aftershocks changed everything. The normal rush of triumph was replaced instantly by something else. Something I don't care to look farther into right now.

I need a drink. A strong one, at that.

"We knew we couldn't trust him," I answer my brother as the ice clinks in the glass. I fill it with three fingers of whiskey and let it sit on the ice to chill. The amber liquid swirls as I consider every aspect of what we could face from Romano.

I know his friends. I know his enemies. And most owe far more to me than they do him.

"Do we need to send anyone a reminder?" I ask my brother as I lift my eyes to his and throw back the whiskey. If anyone wants to prove themselves to Romano, I need to shut down that train of thought before it turns into anything tangible. A small reminder of what we're capable of could silence any ideas anyone has of turning on us. It's best not to entertain any delusions of grandeur they might have.

Jase shakes his head but doesn't return my gaze. Instead, he taps his finger against the back of the chair he's standing behind before continuing. "He messaged Talvery," Jase tells me as the whiskey burns its way down to my gut.

I cock a brow at his statement. "Is that intel from our informant?"

"From one of them," Jase answers with a confidence I respect.

"So, he told Talvery that I allowed his daughter to kill her enemy. That's interesting, isn't it?" I can't hide the amusement that plays along my lips.

"Not exactly. He only confirmed that we have Talvery's daughter."

A sneer of cynicism comes out as a grunt. "Of course, he did," I say absently as I fill the glass once more.

"And then he left a message for us." I don't breathe

or move until Jase tells me, "He says he understands and that he enjoyed the show."

"Fucking prick." I let the words slip out before downing the alcohol in a single gulp. He's a coward. Pitting Talvery and me against one another while pretending to stay by my side. Revenge will be sweet when it comes time for that.

The whiskey is still burning down my chest as my brother asks, "Are we still with him? The guns have shipped. We have the upper hand. We can still pull back from our deal."

"Or side with Talvery?" I ask him and Jase tenses. "We could drop Romano and give the guns to Talvery."

"Why would we do that?" Jase asks with a glimmer of distrust in his voice as he walks closer to me and then settles against the side table, leaning against it and waiting for me to answer. The adrenaline returns full force as if knowing it would be a fatal mistake to put any trust in Talvery. His greed knows no bounds and to aid him could backfire immediately.

I watch the ice in the glass, seeing nothing but Aria. Hearing her pleas to spare her father.

The way she molded her body to mine in the shower was intoxicating. But she's still holding back. I would do anything to have her completely. This could be it.

But the risk is considerable.

Give it time, I hear a voice urge in the back of my head, but it can't be mine. Patience can go fuck itself.

"Of course... Aria." My brother answers his own question given my silence and then runs a hand down the back of his head. It takes him a moment before he reaches for a glass and then takes the bottle of whiskey from my hand.

I let him. I already know she's making me think differently than I should. Making my actions unpredictable. She has a control over me that's undeniable and more and more apparent each day.

"You've never let anyone come between you and business before." He downs the first shot, not waiting for a reply. Sucking the whiskey from his teeth, he asks, "Why her?"

Silence descends upon us. I've never told anyone the complete truth. About how I wanted to die all those years ago. I was so close, and she stopped it.

Before tonight, I hadn't told them that I'd hated her for it. I didn't tell anyone that I'd prayed for it all to end. That at my greatest moment of weakness, I'd given up.

Until she stopped it all.

Jase considers me for a moment. He's my second-in-command. My partner in all of this. And I never told him. I didn't want to speak the truth to life. "I need to know what she means to you at least."

"Everything." I don't hesitate to answer him, although my voice comes out lowly and full of possessiveness.

"And she wants you to side with Talvery. The man who tried to have us all murdered in our sleep? The man who set our house on fire?"

"She doesn't know." I'm quick to defend her and

even I feel the irritation of it. As if it seeps from the tone of Jase's voice straight to my head.

"She doesn't know shit," he responds with slight agitation, but one look at him and he looks away, staring at the liquid swirling in his glass.

"She's loyal."

"She doesn't owe him her loyalty." He finally looks at me. He's not telling me anything I don't know already. "Does she know about her mother?" he asks.

"It's a rumor. We can't prove it." Even as I answer him, I know I'm merely playing devil's advocate. I'd do anything in my power to give her hope for the one thing she wants. Mercy toward her father.

"I'd planned to torture it out of Stephan," I tell my brother, reminding myself. I'd intended to give her truth tonight, along with the vengeance she so desperately needed. "I lost sight of that goal."

Jase only huffs, although when I glance at him there's a shimmer of delight in his eyes and a smirk on his lips before he sips the expensive whiskey.

"She'll never believe me." As I give Jase yet another excuse, I feel a vise around my heart. Squeezing it tight. "She would never side with me over her father." The truth is damning.

"I don't mind telling her." The ease with which he speaks catches me off guard. He must see it in my face though because he shrugs and adds, "I'll be gentle, but I'll make her understand."

"I don't want you getting between us." The rise of anger is something I didn't expect. Clearing my throat,

I return to the whiskey. One more and then I go back to my Aria.

"She's fucking with your head," Jase says with a hard edge before adding, "I've never seen you like this."

"Like what?" I ask him, daring him with my tone to question me. Although, I already know the answer.

"Indecisive and emotional. We should have already annihilated them. You're taking your time and stockpiling more weapons and men than necessary."

"I don't want her to hate me." I expect to see shock in Jase's expression. Maybe even disgust. She's a weakness I never intended, but one I refuse to give up.

Although he's taken aback, he doesn't argue, and a tiredness sets in his dark eyes. The weight of everything I've been feeling is settling down on his shoulders now.

I propose to my brother, "We have to choose. Talvery or Romano."

"I'll die before siding with Talvery," my brother confesses without a hint of emotion. It's merely a fact. And one I can support and respect, given everything Talvery has done. "I'd rather take them both out."

Feeling the heat and buzz of the liquor slinking its way into my thoughts, I merely nod and then roll my tense shoulders. I'm tired. Not just of tonight. But tired of fighting.

There's no way to make it end though. The moment a man stops fighting in this business, is the moment he's executed.

"We've pissed them both off, so it's better to choose a side and make sure they don't put their past behind them to take us on together. Just because Romano slipped him intel doesn't mean anything more than he's fueling the flames between them... but he knows what he's doing. He's redirecting Talvery's hate."

Jase's head falls back as he downs the whiskey and sets the glass down heavily on the tabletop. He breathes out long and low as he nods his head in agreement.

"We can't let that happen. But between the two, Romano is the best choice." He stares at me, making sure I listen to his final words. "You already know that. Siding with Talvery will be the end of us."

He's not wrong. And dropping my gaze, I give in to what I'd already decided. To what I knew had to happen. Romano can't be trusted, but he can be manipulated and used. Talvery would slit our throats the second he got a chance. He's already tried to wipe us out before and failed. And for that reason alone, allowing him any mercy would be a sign of weakness.

Instead of answering my brother, I give him a short nod and turn to leave him, to head back to Aria.

"How is she?" he asks me, changing the subject before I can depart.

"Handling it well, all things considered." The image of her trembling form in the shower reminds me that she's not well. "Today was hard on her. I should go back."

"You should," he says beneath his breath, although he speaks so quietly I'm not sure if the words were meant for me or for himself.

"It had to be done," I remind him, and he nods his head in agreement.

Feeling the conversation is over, I start to leave, but he calls out for me one more time.

"Carter…"

Looking over my shoulder, I see the sincerity in my brother's expression when he tells me, "Be gentle with her."

THE MOONLIGHT FILTERS through the slits in the curtain and washes over Aria's curves, hidden beneath the covers. Her hair is a messy halo, still damp on the pillow as she lies on her side.

My cock instantly hardens, remembering how I left her. Naked and wanting.

She's a good girl, my little songbird, so I know she'll be naked with the exception of my necklace around her throat. She'll be ready for me to take her.

The words from Jase still ring clear in my head. *Be gentle with her.*

Jase doesn't know her like I do, but he knows women far better than I ever have.

The images of me slamming into her and rubbing her clit until she's screaming my name push me to forget Jase's advice. To continue fucking Aria into obedience… until the moment I come closer to her.

She's still trembling. Her hands clutch one another in front of her and her eyes are closed tightly. As if she's praying in the bed.

Her breathing is a mess of stutters.

Not all of us are made to be killers. I knew that

when I gave her the knife and set Stephan up to be her victim.

"It's the adrenaline," I tell her quietly, cutting through the hushed night with my tense words. Her body jolts under the sheets and she stiffens, but her hands and shoulders still tremble.

I watch as she swallows and then her lips part. The look in her hazel-green eyes is a mix of utter sadness and fear.

"I can't stop," she says, and her words are a whisper.

The need to make it all go away rides me hard as I quickly crawl into bed with her, pulling back the sheets and letting her fall into my arms. "Please, help me," she begs me.

"Shh," I hush her, petting her hair and pulling her closer to me. Her small body clutches at mine as if she can't get close enough. "I shouldn't have left you," I whisper out loud and into her hair, feeling the wisps tickle my jaw.

She only responds by moving her hands to my chest and burying her head beneath my chin. She's so frail in my embrace.

Which is anything but the Aria I know.

Maybe I've finally broken her. I already knew I was a monster, but the smile that begs to creep onto my lips at the thought is a validation of that fact. I'm not worthy of a single breath, let alone the woman in my arms.

She's not broken; a woman like Aria can't be broken. A voice whispers deep in the back of my mind, where it hides in the crevices. And the smile that begged to come out before forces its way to my face. I can only hide it by kissing her hair as I rub soothing strokes up and down her bare back.

"You're fine, songbird," I tell her, and I know she can feel the hum of my deep words with her face pressed so firmly against my chest. "It's only the adrenaline."

She doesn't move from her spot, but her lashes tickle my chest as she opens her eyes and then blinks. Her breath is hot and her nails scratch lightly against my skin, but she doesn't ask the question on the tip of her tongue. *How do I know?*

Her hands continue to shake as she attempts to inch even closer to me. With her refusing to let go of me, I reach down and pull the covers tighter around her before telling her my story.

Not all people are made to be killers, but sometimes even the sweetest of creatures have to murder. I may not have ever been innocent, but there was a time when I wasn't the callous and brutal man I am today.

"The first man I killed was a bartender named Dave," I speak quietly without pausing my strokes along her back. Kissing her hair again, I stare at a sliver of light that flits across the bedroom floor. I only know Aria is listening because of the flutter of her lashes again. "I was sixteen," I confess to her as I'm taken back to that night.

"My father didn't deal with my mother's impending death all that well." A huff of ludicrous laughter makes my shoulders shake and her body moves with mine. "He was a coward, I know that now, but to face the deaths of the ones you love... well, I can't blame him for being a coward, but I can blame him for bringing me down with him."

"What happened to your mother?" Aria asks gently, and her soft breathing is steady. It's only then that I see her shaking has turned into a slight tremble.

"She had cancer. It took two years to kill her." The memory makes my chest feel tight, but I continue with the story, the one that makes me angry, not the one that I don't have the strength to face. "My father couldn't stand to see how she deteriorated. So, he drank himself into the man he was without her."

My gaze drops to the comforter. "I swear he was a good man with her, but knowing he was going to lose her changed him." My voice lowers, and I force aside the emotions that come with her memory. To vanish into the back of my mind where they belong.

"One night, my father got himself into trouble and my mother was barely breathing." The image of her on the hospital bed they'd sent to our home for her hospice care causes my voice to crack, but I don't think Aria can hear it.

"He hadn't been home in nearly twelve hours and I knew she wasn't going to make it much longer." He knew too. He had to have known. We were only boys and even we knew she was going to die. "She died while I was away looking for him."

Aria's grip on me loosens, her nails trailing on my chest as her head lifts to look at me. I can feel her gaze on me, but I don't return it.

I can still hear the way the fall leaves crunched

under my sneakers and feel the way the water from the earlier rainstorm seeped into a hole on the bottom of my sole as I trawled through the alleys looking for him.

"He used to go to a few bars I knew." I was young, but the bartenders knew me by name at that point. Aria doesn't stop looking at me, and I feel vulnerable and exposed under her eyes.

She makes me weak.

"I found him in the bathroom, beat up pretty bad. He said it was the bartender. I forget what excuse my father had, but then he cried and said he couldn't move. He cried and that's something he never did. He always drank away his pain. They beat him up and then cuffed him to the radiator, so they could come back and do it again. And again. All the while my mother waited for him."

Aria sniffles against my chest and whispers an apology.

As the memories come back to me I tell her, "My father was a poor excuse for a husband. And even a man. But what they'd done..."

I can't explain to her how the anger spurred me on. In the moment that I thought I was going to lose both of them in one night, the anger is what kept me from breaking down.

Licking my lower lip and trying to play off the hoarseness in my voice as anything but emotion, I continue. "The bartender knew my mother was dying. He knew we were on our own. He could have done a lot of things. He could have called the cops to remove my father. He could have locked the doors. But he wanted to humiliate him. He wanted to have a punching bag as payment for the debt my father owed him."

I remember the way Dave looked at me that night when I left my father where he was and walked behind the bar to demand the key. He had a smile on his smarmy face. I knew he was a dick the moment I saw him, from his slicked back hair and the glint in his eyes. I'd heard around town that he liked to get the young women who came to his bar drunk and take advantage of them. I didn't want to believe it though, not when I saw my father laughing with him other nights I'd come to get my drunkard of a father back home.

"I went to get the key and Dave tried to punch me. He was piss drunk. I was only a kid."

"You never should have had to—"

"In the streets where I grew up, it wasn't uncommon, Aria." I cut her off before she can show me sympathy or even begin to suggest that I was too young for what I saw and what I was involved in. I'm not the only one who's gone through this shit and I won't be the last. Everyone leads different lives and there are no pretty promises or mercy for some of us.

"I grabbed the chair and I didn't stop hitting him with it. The other guys there never got up when Dave went after me, but they did come for me. Not at first. Not the first time I struck him with the metal legs. The ring of the metal bashing into his head was louder than the basketball game playing on the one TV in the corner of the bar." Aria remains silent, and I continue.

"They didn't even get up when he fell to the floor. I

didn't stop cracking his head in with the chair. I couldn't." A lot like Aria tonight. I hadn't made the connection until the thought hit me.

I remember how I didn't even think I was breathing. I didn't think it was real. I didn't want it to be.

"I didn't kill him that night," I tell her and then kiss her hair. My grip on her shoulder tightens and I pull her back into my chest. "The other assholes there dragged me away from him, but the minute I was free, they let me go. I got my father after leaving Dave on the floor bloodied up and moaning."

I can see each of their faces now, full of fear and disbelief that a scrawny boy had nearly killed the man on the floor. My chest heaved but the adrenaline took over.

I killed him a week later after my mother had died and we'd buried her. He came to get money to cover the hospital bills for his broken nose. Money we didn't have, but he expected we would from the life insurance that didn't exist.

No one else was home and I wasn't supposed to be home either, but the guilt of leaving my mom that night kept me from going anywhere for days.

My mother died while I was gone, and I know if I had to put the blame somewhere, it should be on my father.

I know that Dave wasn't the reason that my mother died. But as he stood in the doorway of our home, telling me that the life insurance money from my mother's death was going to him, I lost it. I already knew there was no life insurance. There was no money. There was no helping my father, a man who didn't want to be helped. There was no bringing my mother back.

I knew all of that. I also knew that the man in front of me didn't care.

He didn't care about any of that. And so, I let him into our home, grabbing the pistol my father kept by the door as I closed it. I walked Dave into the kitchen where my mother died on the hospital bed under the pretense of retrieving the check sitting on the counter. I shot him in the back. Just once, with shaking hands. But once was enough.

I didn't stop shaking, not even hours after Sebastian had helped me throw Dave's body into the river. He was the only friend I had and the only person I could turn to. He was older than me, stronger than me and he was there for me when I had no one. He didn't stay for long though. He had his own demons to run from, and plenty of them.

I couldn't stop shaking. If it wasn't for my brothers, I don't think I could have continued living. In a way, it was our first act together that led to this empire. Nothing can bring you closer to someone than death can.

I remember how I didn't want to bury Dave like Sebastian suggested because I couldn't stand to see upturned dirt after watching my mother being lowered into the ground only days before. I threw up as Sebastian dug a hole. I couldn't take it. I couldn't deal with what I'd done and what I was capable of.

And so, we tossed the body in the bed of the truck

instead after covering the partially dug shallow grave, and Sebastian disposed of the body in the river. All while I uselessly rocked myself in the passenger seat of the truck, loathing myself and what I'd done.

"When did you kill him?" Aria asks me, breaking up my thoughts and bringing me back to her. I blink away the memories and the heavy sadness in the pit of my chest.

It takes me a minute to realize I hadn't voiced the last bit of my story. She thinks I just lost it at the bar. She doesn't know that I did it days later and that I led him into the house knowing I wanted to see the man die.

"Does it matter when he died?" I ask her, wanting to keep the truth from her and thinking that it makes it better if it was just heat of the moment. But nothing makes being a murderer better.

She doesn't answer me, she only lowers her cheek to my chest and I continue holding her, remembering how I shook that night after ditching Dave's dead body into the river. "The shaking will stop," I whisper.

Time passes slowly, neither of us speaking until I finally feel the weight of the day and tell Aria to sleep.

"I don't want to sleep," she tells me wearily and then forces herself to swallow. "I'm afraid I'll see him. He'll be there waiting for me."

"Shh," I hush her again, cupping her chin in both of my hands and gently placing a kiss on her forehead. I notice then how calm her body is.

It's amazing what a distraction can do to a person. It can make you forget about everything.

"He's gone," I remind her, although her prolonged fear worries me.

Killing him was supposed to set her free.

It will, the voice hisses and calms the worry creeping up on me. Nodding as if in agreement with the voice, I kiss her once more, pressing my lips to her smooth skin and then pull back, waiting for her to look at me.

"I told you. All you have to fear is me."

Aria's hazel eyes are deep with emotion, swirling with an intensity that pulls me in and pins me down until her lips part and my gaze drifts to them.

The yearning to press my lips to hers nearly wins, but instead, I remember yet another aspect of tonight that I'd planned and forgotten about.

"Wait here," I command her, and disappointment causes her gaze to lower, but she releases me for the first time since I'd crawled into bed to be beside her.

As I walk to the dresser, I strip off my shirt and pants before grabbing the case with a syringe in it and a bottle of oil from the drawer. I haven't needed it for so long, but she needs it tonight. It will let her sleep if nothing else.

Standing next to the bed, I motion for her to come to me before telling her to turn around and get on all fours. I've come to expect a lot of things from Aria. Her sass and her mouth, her questions, and defiance.

But tonight, all she does is obey, and that stirs up something inside of me. Both the pure and the depraved desires. She doesn't even ask why.

My hand gentles on the curve of her ass then moves

up to her waist and back down before I give her the shot, making her jump slightly before she steadies herself and then I can push down the plunger of the syringe.

"Birth control," I tell her and then smirk at the thought as I add, "it's better late than never."

Aria only murmurs a response, placing both her hands flat on the sheets and her cheek follows as she turns her head.

"I have this for you too," I tell her after setting the empty syringe down on the nightstand and pushing on her hip. "Sit up," I command her, and she obeys easily, wincing slightly as her ass presses against the comforter.

"It should help you sleep," I explain as I pull the liquid into the bulb syringe. The oil is clear, a pure drug that will hit her hard the first night. "Have you ever heard of Sweet Lullabies?" I ask her, and she tilts her head with a crease in her forehead indicating her confusion.

"Lullabies? I know a few-"

"No, the drug."

I don't expect her to. We've only just started selling the adapted version that's marketable. She shakes her head, proving me right although the confusion in her expression stays in place.

I lift the syringe to her lips and she obediently opens her mouth, tilting her head back slightly for me. I admire how the moonlight reflects off her slender neck and plays with the shadows down her body as the liquid hits her tongue.

"Suck it down." The command I give her makes my dick stir, but she'll be out soon. Within minutes, I would bet.

"What is it?" she asks me, and I debate on telling her how it came to be and how it's responsible for so many of the reasons I am who I am, but she yawns, cutting me off before I begin.

"Just lie down," I tell her gently, and pull back the covers for her to nestle in beside me. I've had her in my bed a number of nights now, but she's never readily slept this close to me.

With the rustling of the sheets silenced, I let my hand rest on her hip and rub soothing circles there. I breathe in the scent of her hair and leave a small kiss there as I listen to her steady breathing and know that sleep has taken her before I could even begin to admit what this drug really is.

CHAPTER 5

Aria

I USED to dream of things I'd bet all girls dream about.

I would dance so beautifully, my hair swinging in the air as I landed a perfect pirouette. In my dreams, I could be and do anything. I'd dance in a ballet center stage, and amidst a crowd of thousands, I'd perform beautifully.

I'd climb the mountains and find a magical field of flowers where they came to life like the story of *Alice in Wonderland*. I could talk to the animals and drink tiny cups of tea that would make me small enough to follow the rabbits down the rabbit holes.

I could be anyone I wanted to in my dreams. But those visions were from long ago. It's funny how they come back tonight.

Each of the scenes flashes through my head as if on fast forward. I see myself as a young girl performing the arts I wanted to before I realized my insecurities would keep me from even trying. I watch as I remember a dream I had of kissing a boy in my class. I imagined my leg would kick up behind me as he deepened it.

But even as the memory of my dreams from long ago comes to life before me, I'm aware that they're only dreams. I never kissed Paulie. I never had the courage to and if I had, I know it wouldn't have happened the way I pictured it.

For a moment, I question if I'm dreaming or awake. Everything is so vivid. So real.

But the scenes keep going. They don't stop for me.

The hairs at the back of my neck prick as I know what's coming. They're all in order, like a timeline of my hopes as I watch the scenes play out. I know I'm getting older. I know what's to come, and I want it to stop.

My head shakes. Make it stop.

But they don't.

I watch as I dream about my mother and me in the park. She's there with her friend like she always is. And I'm there drawing instead of playing with the other girls. I dreamed of drawing something that day, but when I look down at the paper it's blank. I can't remember what it was. But it doesn't matter. All I can focus on is her face. This is the dream that turned into a nightmare. The first dream of so many I had over and over again.

Make them stop. My throat closes, and I want to scream. It's too real, too vivid. And I can't stop it.

I can feel my nails digging into the sheets. I'm awake, but I can't open my eyes. I can barely move, and I can't stop the images.

My heart races as I see myself in the closet.

Please stop, I whisper in my dreams, but my throat doesn't feel the words. Not like my chest feels the pounding of my blood.

There she is standing with her back to me, facing the door. My mother's standing there and I'm terrified. Why did she tell me not to leave? Not to scream. Not to move except to hide.

Terror races through my veins.

I wish I could move and go to her. To help her.

Please make it stop. I don't want to see it again.

I don't want to see him push the door open and force her down on the ground. She barely fought him and now I know why.

I can feel the tears leaking down my cheeks and I try to scream, but my words are voiceless.

Stephan looks so young. So much younger than he did when I stabbed him. When I murdered him and put an end to the sick smile on his face.

I can't watch, but I can't close my eyes. I can't turn it off. There's nowhere to run in your dreams.

Please, I don't want to see this. I don't want to remember.

The pain grows in my chest and it paralyzes me. The shaking overwhelms me as he pulls out the knife. It's only a small knife, one like Daddy has for fishing.

Run! I try to scream to myself. *Save her!* I will my limbs to move, but I'm victim to my dreams.

She's still on the ground with her back to him. She's crying so hard but trying not to. She's pinned beneath him as I cover my screams with my hands over my mouth in the closet.

Please, Mom, run, I want to say, but my plea is only a whimper. I know she won't. I have no control here and I've seen this nightmare so many times. The memory haunts me in my waking hours just as much as it does in my sleep.

I didn't know what he was doing to her. Not when he held her down and pushed himself inside of her and not when he pulled out the knife. I didn't know it was over until he sliced her neck open. I knew what death meant and when I saw the bright red blood leaking from her and the way she covered it with her hands as she tried to keep it from flowing, I knew what was happening.

But what he did to her before, I didn't know. It wasn't until a month later when I told my cousin Brett that he explained it to me with a pained expression I'll never forget. I told him everything, but he didn't want to hear. He said Talverys don't cry, we get revenge. He was wrong about both of those things.

Nikolai would listen to me though. He let me cry and didn't make me feel ashamed of that fact.

Even the thoughts of Nikolai don't stop the visions before me. Of my mother with her hair pulled back by Stephan as he slit her throat, of her looking toward the closet where I hid when the life left her.

Her lips are moving.

I can't hear what she's saying.

She's saying something. A chill flows down my arms. This isn't what happens. This isn't what I've dreamed before.

Is this real?

The hairs on my body stand on end. My breath is caught in my throat. I don't watch Stephan like I have before. I know the look of triumph on his face as he wipes off the knife on her bare back. I know what he does next. But my mother is still alive as her face falls to the floor. The blood pools around her cheek like it always does. But this time she blinks slowly and looks at me.

"Mom," I whisper, wanting to move but not able to. *Move*, I will myself hopelessly.

My mom blinks again and she speaks. I know she does. *"I can't hear you, Mom. Please. Please don't die,"* I beg her.

Is this real?

Am I breathing? I can't tell anymore.

I watch her lips, the right side of them covered in her own blood.

But the movement from the man standing behind her steals the attention from her.

Stephan stole what used to be and I can never have it back. Him dying doesn't mean anything.

No, I whisper and shake my head as my small fingers of the child I was, reach out and grab the closet door. I can feel it. I can feel exactly what the edge of the closet door felt like.

My shoulders shake violently; this isn't what happens in my dream. The chill leaves and I feel hot, too hot. "Wake up!" I hear Carter's voice and it begs me to open my eyes, but before they obey, I hear my mother's voice say, "You can't forget me."

I suck in air as my eyes shoot open and I stare at the ceiling of Carter's bedroom through a haze of tears. The lights are bright, so bright it hurts, and I close them just as quickly.

With both of my hands covering my eyes, I feel the wetness and try to rub it all away.

My chaotic breaths are matched with Carter's as I slowly come back to reality. Back to Carter's bed. Back to the safety of this moment and not the nightmare of the past.

It was so real. Again, those goosebumps flood every inch of me as I reach Carter's gaze. His eyes are dark as he stares back at me.

His lips part, but he doesn't say anything for a long moment.

"I was screaming?" I ask him, although I know it's true. My throat feels raw and my words are hoarse.

"For almost half an hour," he tells me with nothing but concern and then visibly swallows as my blood chills. "You wouldn't wake up."

It's been years since I've slept through the entire nightmare. Or even since each second played out as if it were an eternity.

Years have passed, but I know the terror was never like that before.

"I don't know what you need," Carter intimates to

me, sealing me from my thoughts like he's confessing a sin. I watch his throat as he swallows again. Pulling his arms around my chest I try to lie back down as if this is normal. As if this is okay.

"Hold me," I tell him although I stare at the ceiling, seeing the vision of my mother looking at me in the haunted memory. Her still alive on the floor even though I know she was dead.

"Please, just hold me," I plead with him and turn my head, so I can look at him.

Confusion mars his face, but he doesn't say anything. He only climbs closer to me on the bed and pulls me tighter to him.

I need him to hold me more than I've ever needed anything. Other than my mother to come back to me.

CHAPTER 6

Carter

TODAY IS the first day I see Aria as stronger when she's with me. And I can't shake that thought as I enter the den.

I've only left her for a few minutes here and there. Staying quiet behind her and watching her every move. But she knows I'm there and each time she's started to break down, she comes to me.

Of her own free will, she comes to me, asking me to hold her as if my touch could take her pain away.

My poor songbird hasn't realized my touch only brings pain, and I hope she never does.

The drawing pad shows a clean page. Not a mark lays against the stark white.

With a pen in her hand, she lies on her belly on the

rug in front of the fire and stares at the blank sheet as if it'll speak to her.

I would stay there longer, standing behind the sofa, listening to the crackling of the burning wood, and waiting for her fingers to move across the page, but with a shift in my stance, the floor creaks beneath me and breaks her focus.

With lack of sleep, she's slow to move, but she does. Sitting up on her knees she faces me, waiting for whatever it is that I have to say.

It's funny to me how she says when she's with me she forgets, and life is easier.

When I'm with her it's the same until she asks questions, and then I remember everything.

"It's time for the question game again," I tell her, and she drops the pen, letting it roll off her thigh and onto the floor. The frown that's marred her tired expression all day stays in place.

"It feels like forever since we've played this game," she says absently. Her tone, her body language, everything about it is off today. It feels dampened, depressed even. More so than I've seen her before.

Clearing the tension in my throat and letting my hands clench and unclench I remind her, "It hasn't been that long since you've been out of your cell."

A smirk tips her beautiful lips up and she stares at me as if defying the fact. "I said it *feels* like it's been forever... there's a difference."

Her soft gaze trails across the sofa and then back to me. "Am I staying here?"

"You can move wherever you'd like."

"You haven't come near me today like you usually do," she comments and my gaze narrows at her. I recount the day and each and every time she's come to me. The thrill of her choosing to approach me is dulled by the fact that she realizes things have changed between us.

I search her expression for what she's thinking. For a hint as to how this will modify her behavior. But I can't predict her. Not when it comes to what's between us. And thus, it's time for me to question her, to try to gauge what she's thinking based on her own questions.

"That's not a question," is my only reply to her.

She shrugs as if it doesn't matter, and tension spreads through my jaw. "It wasn't my turn to ask," she says simply with a calmness in her voice that only increases the strain.

Be gentle with her. I remind myself again.

Jase offers me a lot of advice though, and my typical response is for him to fuck off. Aria watches me as I walk to the sofa and take a seat on the right side. She decides not to move from her place, but she adjusts to sit cross-legged.

There's a sudden crackle from the fire and she barely acknowledges it. Just like the tension between us.

"How are you feeling today?" I ask her and tell myself it's because I want to get into her head, not because the last twenty-four hours have changed everything.

"Tired," she tells me and the small bit of strength she's shown since I've walked in wanes. She picks at the fuzz on the rug beneath her and answers with a catch in her throat, "I don't know how to feel right now. There's so much..." her voice trails off and I ask her, "So much what?"

The smirk on her face is nothing but fragile as she asks back, "Isn't it my turn?" The walls around her are toppling down. I can see it. I can *feel* it. She's too weak to hold them up any longer, but the girl beneath them isn't what I imagined. She's a girl who's been left alone far too long. A girl who should never have been left alone at all.

And the realization tugs at me like nothing else ever has.

I force my lips into a straight line and give her a small nod.

"Why did you do it?" she asks me in a whisper. Still picking at the imaginary fuzz and only glancing at me occasionally. As if she's afraid to catch my gaze and see something there that could ruin her.

"Do what?" I ask her, although I already know what she's referring to.

Why did I bring her to the dinner? Give her a knife. And let her kill the man who's hurt her so cruelly.

"Why did you... give me the knife?" she finally asks, and her words are twisted and tortured. As tortured as she's been all of today and last night.

"Why did I let you kill him?" I clarify for her, making her come to terms with the truth. She sucks in a heavy breath and pushes the hair from her face as I speak. "Why did I give you a knife so you could kill Alexander Stephan?"

The sofa groans and the fire hisses as I sit back and release what sounds like an easy breath. "Because I wanted you to do it," I tell her and almost elaborate, but the sarcastic huff that spills from her lips as she looks away from me and toward the door stops me from giving her more.

"What did you dream of last night?" I ask her, and I can't help that my body leans forward, eager for her reply. She hasn't been forthcoming, but she always answers me when I give her the opportunity to ask whatever she'd like.

She licks her lower lip, still shaking her head from my non-answer.

"Dreams," she answers with a hint of indignation in her retort. The words I wanted to speak moments before nearly come to life, but then she adds, "I dreamed lots of dreams," shaking her head with the smallest of movements. Her voice is small, and she speaks as if she's not even talking to me.

Like she's validating what she saw with herself.

"It was like my life sped forward in the form of the dreams I had growing up."

My brow furrows as I listen to her. I expected it to be only nightmares with the way she screamed. The memory of her shrill screams and the terror of her cries sends a bite of cold down my back that slowly rolls through every limb.

I couldn't do anything but listen to her and I've never regretted a damn thing in my life as much as I regretted giving her that knife like I did last night while she screamed.

Licking her lips, she continues and then that crease in her forehead returns as she looks at me. "And then I dreamed of the night he killed her."

My head nods on its own. I knew to expect it, that seeing him would elicit those fears for her, but I expected her to be different after she killed him. For the realization that he's dead, to free her in a way she could never be while he was allowed to live.

Give it time, the voice hisses again and the irritation I have for it shows on my face, silencing Aria.

"You can keep going," I tell her, fixing myself and then adding, "if you'd like."

But the moment has passed and instead she takes her turn.

"Are things still the same?" she asks me.

No. The answer is instant and obvious in my head. Strong enough that I feel the word echo through my veins. "Do they feel different?"

"That's not how this game is played," Aria answers with the trace of a smirk on her face although the tiredness has never been so evident in her eyes as it is now. "I asked you first," she tells me and waits for a reply.

"Kneel," I command her, wanting to prove that the power I held over her before is ever present. Even if the fear she held for me has vanished.

The realization that is what's different sends a spike of regret through me, but it's fleeting. I harden my voice as I tell her again, "Kneel and then ask me if things have changed."

The heat ignites in me as Aria narrows her gaze, the

hazel reflecting the flickers of the flames that linger behind her in the fire.

Her lips part and she squirms in her place, but as her eyes close, she only smiles at me while shaking her head.

"I don't want to," she dares to defy me.

My dick hardens instantly, but my knuckles turn white as I grip the arm of the sofa.

Everything inside of me is at war. It seems fitting, since my little songbird seems to be in the same predicament. Her body begging to bend to my command, yet her strong will preventing her from giving in.

"I don't want to punish you today. Not when you need comfort. Don't mistake my gift to you for anything other than what it was." I push the words through clenched teeth, not wanting this tension between us to end. I love her fight. I love it, even more, when I can take it from her.

"And what was it?" she asks me, her eyes sparking with the desire for the truth.

The grin on my face grows as I realize she's set me up, seeking the answer I wouldn't give her when she asked her first question. *Why did I do it?* The tension in my body eases slightly, although the thrill of punishing her is still ringing through me.

"Taking away the fear you had, so I could end it and be the only thing you have left to fear."

"I think you're lying," she bites back although her voice is teasing, sensual even. Not believing me for a moment. Her gaze doesn't waver as she challenges me.

I love that she knows better, but if she knew the power she had over me, I could lose everything. She's still loyal to the enemy. There's no denying that.

The thought makes my gaze drop to the fire behind her and it only returns to her when she adds, "But I don't know why you're lying to me."

"Because you don't need to know," I tell her simply and at first her lips part, ready to tell me off, but then she questions herself.

"You're biting your tongue so hard that I imagine you can taste blood," I point out and try to force a smirk to my lips.

"I've asked you two questions and you haven't answered either truthfully," she tells me and then glances at the fire behind her. "What's the point?" she asks no one in particular with a faint whisper.

"Maybe you're asking the wrong questions," I offer her although my entire body is alive with fire. Yesterday was hard on her and she performed exactly as I wanted, but her defiance today is uncontained, and I have no idea how to handle her. Not when she needs me to give her comfort. I wish I'd had her when I was in this same position years ago.

Even knowing that I've had enough of her insolence.

Those hazel eyes pierce through me at that moment, as if she heard my thoughts. The turmoil inside me twists into a knot until she asks the one question that solidifies my decision to leave her on her own for a few hours, so she can feel the need for me once again.

"Are you still going to let him kill my father?" she asks me. Her voice is steady, with maybe even a hint of provocation there.

Let him.

Let Romano.

She doesn't know that if I could do it myself, I would. If I could be the man to pull the trigger, I'd do it without a second thought.

The silence is only broken by the burning wood, now cracking and hissing. As our conversation continued, the sun has set and with the dimming light from the windows, shadows play along Aria's small form.

"I have to go out tonight."

"That doesn't answer my question," she's quick to reply, not taking her gaze from me.

"The game is over." My voice hardens, the anger pushing through.

She is mine. She will obey. Or I will risk everything to reign over her. There is no question in my mind what will happen if she doesn't take her place beside me.

"How convenient," she responds and that's when I meet my limit. There's only so much she can push.

It only takes three large steps until I'm towering over her. One swift motion and my hand is around her throat. My fingers press against the pulse in her veins as her fingers wrap around my hand. Her eyes widen but not with fear, not even with shock. They widen with hate, with anger... They widen with a spark of fight that rivals the roaring fire behind her.

She's never looked more beautiful to me than she does now.

Her nails dig into my skin, but she doesn't pry them away. She just wants to hurt me. She wants to show me what she's capable of.

Oh, songbird, I already know. She's the one who's only just now realizing what she's capable of.

I lower my lips to hers, deliberately placing a knee between her thighs. Invading every inch of space that separates us.

With the heat of the fire igniting the tension, I whisper against her cheek, "You've forgotten your manners, Aria."

"Manners," she bites out as if the word disgusts her and with the small bit of movement, I squeeze a little tighter. She can breathe, she can speak, but my grip on her is unyielding.

My other hand roams her body, drifting down her waist as I nip along her shoulder and then the fleshy bit of her earlobe. My fingers trace down her thigh and then back up, pulling up her skirt as I move back toward her waist until I let my fingers slide to her inner thigh.

And she moans.

She fucking moans, closing her eyes and letting her head fall back slightly. Even with the fight in her, she craves pleasure more than anything.

"What should your punishment be, songbird?" I whisper against the shell of her ear. The shiver that it ignites in her makes my dick harden to the point that it's painful not to thrust inside of her.

Her answer is a muted moan followed by an attempt to swallow. I don't loosen my grip to aid her; instead, I force her to look at me, to open her eyes and answer me.

"How should I punish this mouth of yours?" I ask her in a low and deep voice, not bothering to contain my desire for her.

"Fuck you," she barely pushes out and then licks her lower lip. Ever the defiant one.

"You would love that, wouldn't you?" I whisper against her lips, letting the words mingle with the heat from the fire and the lust between us.

Her hazel-green eyes swirl with a concoction of everything I know she's feeling. The anger and fear, but more than anything, the longing to be pleasured and cared for.

"Get on your back so I can play with your cunt," I command her the moment my fingers loosen on her throat, nearly making her fall backward. But she catches herself, then lies down as I told her to, one elbow at a time, her eyes never leaving mine.

"You obey so easily when you know you're going to get off, don't you?" I toy with her and the hint of a smirk pulls at the corner of her lips. Her intuition will be our downfall. She thinks she knows who she's playing with. But she doesn't realize what's at stake.

A gentle push on the inside of her thighs has her pulling them apart for me. My pointer trails up the thin black lace of her panties, dampened at her core with her arousal, and then to her swollen clit. Her head falls back, and her nails dig into the threads of the rug as she attempts to hold back the moan that threatens to spill from her lips. I can already hear it though. She's so fucking close. So in need.

"You need to get off. I should have done it last night."

The lace tears easily as I hook my thumb through it, ripping it from her sweet cunt to give me full access to her. With a quick intake of air, she lifts her head to watch me.

All that anger means nothing when I can give her this.

I shove two fingers inside her ruthlessly. Her hips buck and her lower back comes off the floor with the sensation it elicits.

I splay my other hand across her belly and push her back down, not stopping the brutal strokes against the ridges of her front wall.

Her head thrashes and she bites her lip. "Fuck," she says but her plea is only a whimper. Her fingers move to my hand on her belly and then up my forearm. Never stopping, pulling, and searching for something to hold on to.

"Let go," I tell her and for a moment she lets go of my arm, but that's not what I meant. "Give me your pleasure. Let go of everything holding you back from falling," I whisper in the air above her as I watch the light dance across her face. Her lips are parted and make a perfect O although her forehead is scrunched with the strain of holding back her strangled cries of pleasure.

The scent of her arousal permeates the air and

precum leaks from my dick, begging me to slam inside of her.

With my cock pressed against my zipper, I finger fuck her furiously, pushing a third finger inside of her and my thumb against her clit. "I'm not going to stop until you cum on my hand, Aria. I'll fuck you like this until you can't think straight if you don't give me what I want."

Her head thrashes from side to side and then her back bows. I have to push harder with my hand on her hip to keep her down and strum her faster.

"You want another finger?" I ask her and then kiss the inside of her knee. She's so fucking tight I don't think I could though. It's an idle threat, but the idea of stretching her to the point where I could fist her cunt and give her undeniable pleasures she's never felt, has my hand moving harder and faster in unrelenting strokes and I don't stop.

Even as she cries out my name.

Even as her pussy spasms.

Her body rocks with the force of her orgasm and I don't stop, drawing it out and taking every bit of pleasure from her that I can.

It's not until her breath comes back to her and her eyes find mine that I pull away, sucking each of my fingers while she watches.

"Your cunt is so fucking sweet," I tell her and watch her reddened cheeks blush even more violently.

"I'm growing to love your punishments," she says breathily with her eyes closed and the power I feel vanishes. My dick, still pulsing with need, begs me to push her onto her stomach and rut between her legs. She'd cum again. And again.

The worst thing a man of power can do is to issue a false threat. Yet, I've done it with Aria. More than once.

My goal isn't to punish her though; I only want her to obey.

Just as I begin to unbutton my pants, my phone vibrates in my pocket, the timer going off.

Time is up.

With her eyes closed and an angelic look of content on her face, I question leaving her, but I have to.

"Clean up and make yourself dinner." I stifle a groan as I stand, hating that I won't be able to get lost in her touch for hours.

"I'll be back later." I give her the parting words and start to leave. Each movement makes my hard cock ache even worse, but I'll have her tonight.

"Carter?" Aria's soft voice cuts through the air and stops me just as I've started to leave.

"How long will you be gone?" Traces of fear and loneliness linger on her question. This is the new side of her I'm not used to.

The side I've only seen since last night. Back to being the girl behind the broken wall instead of the woman who's angry at being left alone for so long.

"A few hours, maybe."

Her expression falls as she slowly picks herself back up. She only nods in understanding as she covers herself again.

"Do you want anything while I'm out?" I ask her out of instinct, wanting to see her eyes on me again.

Wanting her to show me more of this vulnerability. I can offer her so much more than she ever dreamed.

The very thought spikes awareness through me.

She's the one with control. Topping from the bottom. Sly girl. I need to take it back, for her own good. She needs me to have control, even if she doesn't want to give it to me. Even if she has no idea how much she needs to give it to me.

"No," she answers me with a small shake of the head. "Thank you, though."

"Manners and all," I say to play with her as I leave the room.

Her sweetness numbs the thoughts of demanding more from her, but only so much.

CHAPTER 7

Aria

Hours have passed since Carter left. The smell of garlic is still fresh on my fingers as I head into the dimly lit wine cellar. With a flick and a click, the cellar lights up and a beautiful array of wine bottles shines in the light.

An easy breath leaves me at the thought of getting lost at the bottom of a bottle. One glass or two, and I'll still have my wits with me.

But the wits can go fuck themselves tonight. I don't know what to think or feel. I don't know anything anymore. The memories of what once was and what I am today are playing tricks on my sanity.

I'm acutely aware of it but helpless to do anything about it. That's the worst part.

That, and how I feel about Carter.

It's an ever-changing relationship, but I'm fully aware of the cracked wall between us. He's pretending it's not there, and maybe I'm a fool to think something has changed, but I see the pain and sadness behind his eyes. He can't hide it any longer.

He's broken. It takes a broken soul to know one.

Even what I've been through in only the last twenty-four hours, pales in comparison to how broken and shattered Carter's been for years. And I desperately want to heal him. I want to take his pain away more than I've ever wanted to heal myself.

Deep inside, there's the inkling of some other part of him. If only I could show him.

The pain that claws at my heart only grows at the thought, but with a deep breath I let it all go. I don't know what I am to him anymore. But I care for him regardless, especially after last night.

And until I know what haunts him for sure, there's not a damn thing I can do to change anything. And so, wine it is.

I crouch down at the first row, gripping onto the steel bar of the rack and glancing at each of the labels. Pinot noir. Burgundy. Each of them. I love a good glass of red with spaghetti and Bolognese, and right now, I prefer Cabernet. The next row makes my lips curl up, for the first time in God knows how long.

I can pretend that there's nothing wrong. I can pretend for a short moment. I'm good at doing that. At continuing to go through the motions even though deep inside, I know nothing is okay and there's no way to right the wrongs.

The heavy bottle of dark red wine means I can have a moment. A small, seemingly insignificant moment, to simply breathe.

Well, only while I stay in the kitchen. The thought steals the happiness from my lips and as I stand, I feel my muscles tense once again. At least, until Carter comes back.

When Carter leaves, I'm scared to go anywhere other than the four rooms I'm familiar with. The den, his office, the kitchen, or his bedroom. This place is huge and I'm curious to see more of it. But his brothers are here. Somewhere. *And they're the enemy.*

It's easy to forget when I'm with Carter. He has a compelling power over me. Just being in his presence sets my body on fire and I move with him. Every step, every breath.

But the moment he's gone, I'm so very aware of everything.

"I just need to eat, to drink…" I whisper as I flick off the light and head back with the bottle in my hand to retrieve my dinner from the kitchen island, the aroma wafting to greet me as I shut the door.

But the second I hear the door close, my heart drops at the sound of another person in the kitchen.

"Damn, this smells good," Jase says as he walks closer to the large pot sitting next to the stove. I've already mixed the pasta and meat sauce. He towers over it, picking up the serving spoon and smiling down at my dinner.

My grip nearly slips on the bottle; my palms are so sweaty.

"You make enough for all of us?" he asks me with a charismatic smile.

A truly charming expression graces his face. With his stubble growing out longer than I've seen before, he looks different, but the similarities between him and Carter are still striking.

I can feel myself swallow before I attempt to answer him, but just the sight of him reminds me of last night. I can see him sitting in the chair to my left, smiling while my gaze drifts back to Stephan.

My heart pounds in my chest like it did last night in the shower. I can feel the anxiety and adrenaline mix and it takes everything in me to stand up straight.

"Whoa," Jase says as the spoon hits the steel pot and he practically jogs around the island to come closer to me. As soon as I register that's what he's doing, I instinctively take a step back, my shoulder hitting the closed cellar door. Every time I blink, I see Stephan. Sitting at the table, glancing between Carter and me. Waiting for me to kill. Waiting for me to become a murderer.

He knew. They all knew. And they let Romano walk away.

With both hands raised, Jase widens his eyes and slows his steps, even dropping his stance a few inches and crouching down. "You look a little dizzy," he says softly. "You already have a bottle?" he asks me and to my disbelief, a short huff of a genuine laugh leaves me.

Of course, he would think that I'm drunk and that's

why seeing him would cause me to react with significant panic.

It's not that I saw him only last night, a few rooms away as I murdered a man who'd haunted me for years and continues to do so. It's not that I'm still forced to stay here even though I so badly wish I could run home and hide in my room from all the terrors that plague me. My body heats with anxiety, but the knowledge that I have a grasp on the present gives me much needed strength.

He takes another step closer and I shake my head, pushing off of the door and going around Jase. One of my hands grips the neck of the bottle, the other runs through my hair. "I'm just having a moment," I finally answer him weakly although my back is to him as I walk back to the counter where my wine glass is.

My heart races again. It won't fucking stop. Off and on all day, it's been like this. *I need Carter.* The bottle hits the counter hard and it's only then that I risk a look over my shoulder at Jase.

Jase's eyes are narrowed and he's still standing where I left him. I can't take my eyes away from his as he pins me in place with his gaze. Much like Carter does, but Jase is assessing me.

I have to give him something, but all I can think of is to answer his earlier question. Whether or not I made enough food for everyone else.

"I made the entire package, so there's definitely enough." With the answer coming out easily, I turn back to the wine and opener. Easily uncorking it as I talk to him although I can feel my hands start to tremble again, and my heart threatens to trot out of my chest.

"I wasn't sure if anyone would want a plate, but I was going to save it for leftovers if not." I can hear Jase walk back toward the pot slowly, even though he's still assessing me. The second the wine glass is full, I lift it to my lips.

"So, wine is your therapy?" Jase asks as he stalks over to stand only a few feet from me but leans his lower back against the counter.

"We all have our vices," I offer him and lick my lips. The sweet taste offers little aid to the chaos coursing through my blood. But his soft expression does something to me. It loosens something hard and sharp that was lodged deep inside of my chest, suffocating me.

"I get it," he tells me, his forehead smoothing as he turns and reaches for another glass in the cabinet. "Mind if I have one?"

The shake of my head is weak, but not because I don't want to share. I don't mind at all, especially, if it will give me a chance to win over Jase. I remember a thought I had that feels like forever ago, a thought about using Jase to gain my freedom. Or maybe to ask for mercy for my family.

No, the shake of my head is weak because Declan joins us, striding in as if I called a meeting.

Jase stands beside me, glass in hand as Declan takes Jase's former spot, repeating the motion Jase did when he first walked into the kitchen. "Oh, damn," he says over the pot with a reverence in his voice. "You made us dinner?" Declan asks with a boyish grin.

That's not exactly the truth, but I don't deny it. "I wasn't sure if you'd like it, but there's plenty."

Declan grabs the plates, the clinking ceramic filling the room as Jase gives me space, walking to the other side of the U-shaped island and leaning against it, opposite me. The thought of being in the room with Carter's brothers scared me literally only minutes ago. But an ease washes over me as I watch Declan make a plate and then point the spoon to Jase, who answers the unspoken question.

"Yeah, I want one, I haven't eaten yet."

I lean forward a little off the counter, ready to ask him to make me a plate too, but Declan speaks first.

"You didn't poison it, right?" Declan asks with a shit-eating grin. "You know I've got to check," he jokes and then makes Jase's plate.

And there goes the sense of ease and the smile that graced my lips. It washes away like a lone shell on the shore before the tide.

I'm still the enemy. I will always be the enemy. And that's what they'll always be to me.

I offer him a tight smile and force down the well of sadness and pity. "Not yet, you got here too soon." A tight knot forms in my throat, but I drown it with the wine as Declan chuckles, still piling spaghetti onto the plate. Bastard tears prick at my eyes and all I can think is that I wish either Carter were here or that I was back at home, under the comfort of my blanket.

"I don't think she's eaten yet," Jase tells Declan in a tone that has no trace of the humor I forced into my response. He grabs the two plates Declan's made and motions for me to follow him to the small table to eat in the kitchen. Declan looks shocked at Jase's reaction and the seriousness in his tone and objects to him taking both plates, one of which was his. His forehead creases with confusion... until he sees me.

I've always been shit at hiding what I'm feeling. My father used to tell me I'd fare better in this world if I could learn to lie.

My body moves unwillingly to follow Jase, but at least I grabbed the bottle. I can't look at Declan as he watches me. I know he sees through the faint humor I veiled my emotions with in my response.

"Are you okay eating here?" Jase asks. The legs of the chair make a scratching noise on the floor as he pulls it out for me. I stare at the chair for a moment, marveling at the kindness while questioning his intentions.

He feels bad for me. That's all I can think. He's being nice because I'm wounded. That's all this is.

"I'd rather be alone," I finally answer him, finding my voice and feeling the cords in my neck tensing as I look back at him. I have to force my words out of my dry throat and they hurt as I do. "I just need to be alone for a moment." My breath shudders and the back of my eyes prick as I see the visions of last night again. Only three rooms down. The grand dining room is only three doors down from here.

"Please," I say quickly in a whisper and place the wine down on the table with as much grace as I can.

With both hands on the table, he looks over his

shoulder and says something to Declan, but I don't hear what.

"You going to be okay?" he asks me as I hear Declan's footsteps leaving the kitchen.

"How long does it take to be okay after murdering someone? Even if you feel it was justified in every way?" I ask Jase and he merely looks past me at Declan's exit before bringing his eyes to mine.

Jase doesn't answer me; he simply looks back at me as if I hadn't spoken at all.

I start to think he'll leave me like that, taking his plate with him, but instead, he asks me his own question, "You want me to grab another bottle?" to which I can only nod in response.

He's kind enough to grant me both the loneliness and the second bottle I desire.

CHAPTER 8

Carter

You were supposed to be gentle with her.

Agitation leaves me in a singular deep groan. I don't respond to Jase's text and I don't intend to. He doesn't recognize the severity of the situation. He doesn't know shit about her.

He doesn't know what she needs.

The bitter thought stays with me as I shut down my phone and quietly enter the kitchen. I know she's still sitting where she was an hour ago and just as I expect, she doesn't see me come in.

She never does. She always gives me the opportunity to watch her, to see what she's like when she doesn't know I'm looking.

I'm hardly ever disappointed, but watching as she

fills her glass again, the pleasure of being in her presence again is dulled.

It's becoming a crutch. If she knows I'll be gone, she drinks. It's only happened twice, but still, I notice. Part of me recognizes her condition. Her situation. I realize it may be easy for her to give in to a vice and let herself slip somewhere where the pain is absent, and the choices are meaningless. But I don't want it to become a habit.

With a twist of her finger, she pulls my necklace she wears up closer to her lips, letting the diamonds and pearls play there in between sips of wine and absent-minded hums.

Her lips part slightly as she sways in her seat and stares at a black and white photograph that's in the hall. She hums against the gemstones and I wish I knew what she was thinking. The sadness and tortured stare tell me she's still there, my little songbird with clipped wings.

I don't recognize the song that she hums. I never do. Sometimes it sounds more like a conversation than a song.

I follow her gaze as I walk closer to her; the black and white photograph is a picture of the side of our old house. The one that burned down. The one that *her father* had burned down, expecting the four of us to be inside and sleeping.

I feel a sudden pinch along the edge of my heart, reminding me the damn thing is there.

"What are you thinking?" I ask Aria, ignoring the pain in my chest and causing her to jump from the tone of my deep voice.

Her expression is soft, as are her eyes when she turns in her seat. There's even the hint of happiness on her lips.

"You're back," she says and there's a lightness in her statement. She can't hide the relief that slurs with her words. And that bit of disappointment I have at her drunkenness returns.

"I said I'd be back tonight." It's all I offer her as I pull out the chair next to her, letting the feet drag across the floor noisily.

"What were you doing?" she asks me with a pleasantness that seems genuine.

She's naïve to think I do anything pleasant this late at night.

I was ending the life of a thief. A drug addict who bought more and more of SL and wouldn't answer a simple question.

What was he doing with it?

It's a rare day that Jase can't get a response from someone. He's good at what he does. He left the junkie to bleed out and waited for me to come. It's my name they fear the most.

If pain and the threat of death can't get an answer, true fear is quick to provide one.

And it did. The only word the prick spoke before life slipped from him was a name. *Marcus*. All I got was a name. But it was all I needed.

It's a name I'm growing to despise more and more as the days go by. Daniel used to have a good reputation with Marcus, a man who lives in the shadows and never shows himself. But that was before he found Addison again. Since then Marcus has yet to be found, but apparently, he's been busy.

"Work," I answer, and my short response tugs her smile down.

"There are leftovers," she offers me even though the smile's vanished. I can feel how the sweetness inside of her has hollowed out.

As she reaches across the table to play with the stem of her glass I ask her, "You made me dinner?"

"If you didn't all look so alike, I'd know you are brothers by the way you react to a damn meal," she offers with a somewhat playful nature.

I can't pin down what she's thinking. Or what she thinks of me as I stare at her.

"It's been a long time."

"Since you've had Bolognese?" she asks as if my words are nonsense.

"Since someone's made us dinner," I tell her and think of my mother. Once again, Aria looks at me as if she's read my mind. The pretending to be happy and acting like things are normal slips away.

"I'm sorry," she whispers, and I choose not to respond. Sorry doesn't take anything back.

"I like to cook," she offers after a moment, breaking up the silence and tension. "If you'd like… I don't mind cooking more?"

I used to avoid the kitchen and dining room when my mother got sick. It's where she died. None of us liked to go to the kitchen. It was better to be in and out of that room as fast as we could. In a way, I should be thankful Talvery burned that house down. It was nothing but a dark memory.

Her slender fingers move up and down the glass and I expect her to drink it, but instead, she pushes it toward me. "Would you like some?"

I shake my head without speaking, wondering if she knows what I think about her habit.

"I don't like it when you're gone," she says before pulling the glass toward her again.

"Why's that?" I ask her, grateful to talk about anything other than the shit going on outside of this house. Enemies are growing in number each day.

"I start thinking things," she says quietly, her gaze flickering between the pool of dark liquid in the glass and my own gaze.

"Is that right?" I ask her, pushing for more.

"It's better when I don't have a choice," she admits solemnly. "At least, for the way I feel about myself."

"What's better?" The question slips from me as a crease deepens in my forehead.

"My thoughts are better," she states but doesn't elaborate.

"How's that?"

"If I'm with you, I don't worry about my family, the fighting..." her voice cracks and her face scrunches. "That's awful, isn't it?" She shakes her head, her flushed skin turning brighter. "It's horrible. I'm horrible." And with her last word she picks up the glass, but I press my hand to her forearm, forcing the glass back down to the table.

"You're many things," I tell her evenly as I scoot the seat closer to her, "but horrible isn't one of them."

"Weak. I'm weak," she answers with disgust on her tongue. Her gaze leaves mine, although I will her not to break it. Instead, she stares at the stem of the wine glass. There's still a good bit in her glass, but from what I can tell, this is her second bottle. "I'm so weak that I want to have no choice," she says disbelievingly. "How fucked up is that?"

"You're in a difficult position, with few options and severe consequences." I've never been good with comfort, but I can offer reason. "And deep down inside, you know whatever you do, it won't change anything." The truth that flows easily from me is brutal and it causes Aria to visibly cower from me.

"Thank you oh so much," she says with a deadpan voice as she lifts the glass and then downs all the remaining alcohol. "I was beginning to feel pathetic and like my life had no meaning whatsoever." She raises her hand in the air and then slaps her palm down firmly on the table. There's a bite of anger to her words that pisses me off. The glass hits the table before she looks me in the eye and tells me with an expression devoid of any emotion but hate, "Thank you so much for clearing that up for me."

"I do enjoy your fight, Aria. But you'd be wise not to speak to me like that." My own voice is hard and deadly, but it does nothing to Aria.

"Would I now?" A simper graces her wine-stained lips. "I'm not sure there's a single wise thing I could do, is there, Mr. Cross? Other than obey your *every* command."

Her defiance is fucking beautiful and only makes me hard for her. My cock stiffens and strains against my zipper as I lean back to take her in. It feels as if we're picking right back up where we left off and I couldn't be more agreeable with that situation.

My breathing quickens as she stares at me, daring me to disagree with her.

"You love being angry, don't you?" I ask her, although it's not a question. "There's so much more power in anger than there is in sadness." The statement makes her lips purse.

"You have no idea what you're capable of," I tell her a truth that could destroy me. "Women like you were made to ruin men like me."

"Oh?" she asks. "Us women who aren't capable of changing anything?" She seems to remember her fight as she adds, "You'll have to clear that up for me. I'm either too drunk or stupid to understand."

"Or too blinded by your past?" I offer her. "So consumed with changing something that's meant to happen. That *will* happen, so much so that you can't see what lies ahead."

"What's meant to happen? As in?" she questions as she noticeably swallows. Her hands grip the edge of the table as if she needs to hold it in order to sit upright.

"You know exactly what I mean, Aria."

"If it happens, if what I think you're referring to right now happens, there will be no future for me. The willing whore of the enemy who could do nothing to save the people she loves. What kind of life is that to lead?"

My blood runs cold at her words. Numbly I watch her reach for the remains of the bottle closest to her, only to find it empty.

Would she kill herself? Is that what she's saying? My blood pounds in my veins at the thought of her leaving me, let alone leaving me in such a manner. I can barely look at her as she sags back into her seat and turns to give me her attention again. "If you were me, what would you do?" she asks with genuine curiosity.

I'm still reeling from her earlier confession to answer quickly, but I finally find words that have a ring of truth to them. "I'd take care of myself and my own survival."

"My own survival?" she asks with a sarcastic huff of disbelief. "If they're dead, then who am I?"

My breathing becomes ragged, tense, and deep at her question. "You are mine." My answer is immediate, stern, and undeniable. Each word is given with conviction.

But all they do is turn her eyes glossy. "And that's all I'll ever be. A possession."

The sadness is what destroys my composure. She unravels me like no one else ever has. She'll devastate everything I worked for, everything I am, but so long as I have her, it will all be worth it.

"I was meant to have you. I only fucking lived to have you." I've never spoken truer words.

Her breathing is shallow as her chest rises and falls. "Carter?" She says my name as if I'll save her from what she's feeling, from the truth breaking down every bit of her own beliefs.

"You were made for me to have. To fight. To fuck. To care for," I say as I lean closer to her, my grip tightening on the back of her chair as I lower my lips until they're just an inch from hers. My eyes pierce into hers as she stares back at me with a wildness I crave to tame. "Do you understand that, Aria?"

"You're a very intense man, Carter Cross." She speaks her words softly with tears in her eyes that I don't understand.

All I can do at this moment is crash my lips to hers, to silence the pain, the agony, all of the questions she has. The kiss isn't gentle; it isn't soft and sweet. It's a brutal taking of what's mine. What's been owed to me for years.

The instant I capture her lips, she gasps, and I shove my tongue inside of her mouth, pushing myself out of the chair and hearing it bang on the floor as I take her face with both of my hands. My tongue strokes hers swiftly and she meets my intensity with her own. Her fingers spear through my hair and her nails scratch at my scalp, pulling me to get impossibly closer.

She moans in my mouth as I pull away, desperate to breathe. In one movement, I pull her down to the floor while shoving her skirt up her thighs, maneuvering her beneath me. Her belly presses to the floor and my erection digs into her exposed ass.

"You're such a dirty girl, not bothering to cover this." I cup her already wet pussy as I ask her, "Aren't you?"

My other hand grips the hair at the base of her skull and pulls back hard enough to make her back bow. Her lips part with a sweet gasp of both pleasure and pain as I ruthlessly rub her clit.

"You're mine, and nothing else. You'll let go of everything but what I command you to do and be." My words are whispered against the shell of her ear. They mingle with her moans as I stare at those gorgeous lips. Desperate to take them again, I give in to what I want. Removing my hand from her cunt, I grab her throat from behind and crash my lips against hers.

"Carter," she heaves my name the moment I break the kiss and without thinking twice, I release my cock and slam inside of her.

Feeling her hot, wet walls spasm the moment I enter her drives me insane. She's so fucking tight, but she takes all of me to the hilt with a strangled cry.

My hips piston with a relentless pace to claim her and everything she is. Everything she'll ever be.

"Mine," I grunt out and release her throat and hair to grip her hips with a bruising force.

Her arms barely bracing her as she cries out her pleasure.

Over and over I fuck her as hard as I can. And each one of her strangled moans, combined with her hopeless scratching at the floor beneath her, only fuels me to fuck her harder.

"Mine." I push the word through my teeth as she cums violently beneath me. My own release follows, my balls drawing up and my toes curling as thick streams of cum fill her pussy.

She lies there panting, her small body sagging as she desperately tries to support herself and breathe at the same time. Both efforts seemingly in vain.

My cum leaks out of her as she whispers my name again and again. Bracing one forearm on each side of her, I rake my teeth up her neck and nip her chin before kissing her again.

And she kisses me back, reverently and sweetly. Her hands find my chin and her fingers brush along my scruff to keep my lips pinned to her own.

My chest heaves in air as I fall to the floor next to her.

The cool air relieving my heated skin.

The only effort Aria makes is to inch closer to me, to have both her bare and clothed skin touching mine.

"I've been waiting for that," she says softly as she nuzzles next to me, content with being held.

"For what?" I ask her, still catching my breath.

"For you to kiss me like that."

To kiss her. The memory of her lips hot on mine begs me to kiss her again, but her words stop me.

"It was worth the wait." The words fall easily from her lips, the same lips that look swollen and reddened from our kiss.

The reality comes back to me in this moment.

This isn't what this was supposed to become.

I don't know what the fuck she's doing to me, but it can't continue like this.

I'm ruining everything.

CHAPTER 9

Aria

I'M SURPRISED I slept as well as I did.

No terrors, just a much-needed deep sleep. From whenever Carter brought me to bed, until nearly 2 p.m. this afternoon.

There isn't enough sleep to mend the exhaustion I feel, but I'm grateful I've gotten through one night undisturbed.

As I shift on the wooden floor in Carter's office, the ache in my muscles intensifies and I wince. I'm so fucking sore from last night. From this whole past week, maybe. I don't know if this is normal or not, but I hurt. Every moment of the day, I feel him inside of me still and it takes me to the edge of both pleasure and pain.

Both physically and emotionally.

There's no denying Carter is a broken and lost soul. And there's no denying that I want to make all the wrongs in his past right.

My mind is a whirlwind of what I wish could be undone, but there are no answers that take pity on me and provide me with clarity. All I can think to do is offer him kindness. To obey, to be good for him. And maybe he'll feel something other than the anger and hate that cloud his judgment.

I can only imagine the world he grew up in. The small pieces I've been given are jagged and harsh.

I shouldn't pity the monster he became.

I shouldn't love what he does to me.

But I do.

The short piece of chalk rolls back and forth between my fingers as I study the paper lying on the floor. I can't remember what I drew at the park. The questions I had in my dream from not last night but the night before, are still alive and vibrant in my mind.

I can't help but to think there are answers in my subconscious. Answers in my dreams.

But I can't remember what I drew that day.

Instead, I keep drawing the same thing, the house from the photograph in the hall. It's quaint and small, with rustic features. It's definitely a backroad setting but there are other houses beside it. Close to each other.

The brick was old, and the mortar seemed even older. The weeds that grew up the side of it felt as if they belonged there like nature was intent on reclaiming the structure.

Whoever took the photograph captured the beauty of the home perfectly, but why does it call to me? Why do I keep drawing it and only changing the flowers that grow around it?

"There are four steps." Carter's voice breaks into my thoughts and I glance up at him, not registering his words. He takes his time rolling up the crisp, white sleeves of his dress shirt. I can't help but admire the corded muscles under his tanned skin and remember how his hands gripped me last night, leaving bruises on my hips that still ache to the touch.

He gestures to the drawing. "The front porch had four steps."

It takes me a moment to comprehend and I offer him a small smile before asking him, "This was your house, wasn't it?"

He nods and adds, "You make it seem more alluring than it was."

My heart tugs and a small knot forms in my throat as he returns to his laptop. Maybe if he grows to care for me, everything can be okay. It can be made right.

What a naïve thought.

"What are you thinking?" Carter's question brings me back to the present again.

"I keep drifting into thoughts I shouldn't," I answer him without much conscious consent. Maybe I've rested so much that the sleep refuses to leave me, making me drowsy and my thoughts hazy.

"Like?" he prompts.

"Like, wondering why I love this house so much," I answer him cautiously although my gaze stays on the paper.

"I hate that house," Carter says after a moment and I move my eyes to his. The coldness in his eyes is ever present and it sends a chill down my spine.

"You hate everything," I tell him absently.

"I don't hate you," he says pointedly, and his rebuttal sends a warmth flowing through me.

"How do you feel about me then?" I ask him and busy my fingers with the piece of chalk.

His words are softly spoken and it's the first admission from him of any kind. "The very idea that you're mine makes me feel as if there isn't a thing I can't conquer. But actually having you is... everything."

I don't know if he realizes how powerful his words are. How intense he is. Just being around him is suffocating. Nothing else can exist when he's with me.

"What do you remember about last night?" he asks me, and I blink away the trance he held over me.

"Everything," I answer him as if it's obvious. "You came home. We had a conversation and then more on the kitchen floor..." I trail off and my teeth sink into my bottom lip at the memory. "And then you took me to bed."

Carter nods slowly as if gauging my response. "You don't remember what you told me when we got to bed? Do you?" My heart flickers once, then twice as I try to remember.

But I don't.

"I fell asleep," I tell him as if it's an excuse.

It's quiet for a long moment and an uneasiness washes through me. Like I've said something that I should regret but I don't know what it was. Swallowing thickly, I steel myself to ask, "What did I say?"

But he doesn't answer me, he only tsks in response.

A pounding in my chest and blood makes me feel on edge until Carter rises and stalks toward me. He looms over me, owning me with his presence as he likes to do. My eyes close as he lowers his hand to the crown of my head gently and then twirls a lock of hair between his fingers.

My heart races with his touch and I don't know if it's from fear or lust.

"All I want to do is fuck you until there's no question in your mind who you belong to." His admission forces my thighs to clench and that tender ache returns.

The tension and fear dissipate with each small touch he gives me.

"If you gave yourself to me, everything else would fall into place."

His fingers trail lightly along my collarbone and up my chin then move to my lips, tracing them with a tender touch that I would have once found difficult to believe belongs to Carter.

"Is that all? Just give myself entirely to you to use as a fucktoy? That would solve everything?" My comeback is weakened by the gentle way the words flow, the flirtation that I can't deny in their cadence.

His cock is right in front of my face, obviously hard

and pressing against his pants. My mouth parts and my fingers itch to reach out and take him.

The throbbing between my thighs intensifies and I struggle to remind myself that I'm his captive, his fuck-toy, his whore, and nothing more. All I can think is how much I want to pleasure him like he did me last night.

I want to bring him to his knees and make him weak for my touch like I am his.

"I want to..." I have to stop myself and swallow my words, feeling dirty.

He crouches in front of me, his gaze penetrating mine with an intensity that begs me to lean away from him, to run from the beast of a man who isn't hiding anything from me.

His darkly said words are whispered from his lips. "Tell me what you want, Aria."

"I- I-" I stutter. Like an insignificant unequal.

It takes every ounce of courage in me to raise my gaze to his, to inhale a breath, and on the exhale confess, "I want to suck you."

"You want to wrap these pretty little lips around my cock until I cum in the back of your throat?" he asks easily with a huskiness that comes from deep in his chest, moving his pointer to my lips and tracing them once again.

I nod, forcing his finger to alter its path and graze against my cheek instead. I'm breathless, full of desire and want, numb to everything but him.

What has he done to me?

The thought hits me as he leaves me panting on the

floor to grab one of the chairs in front of his desk and move it directly in front of me. He wastes no time, performing the task quickly.

He doesn't speak as he sits down, both of his hands resting easily on his thighs.

My hand is shaky as I lift it to his zipper, but he catches me before I touch him. His grip is hot and demanding and steals my attention and breath just the same.

I'm pinned by the lust in his eyes as he asks me, "Have you done this before?" He tilts his head to ask, "Have you done anything before me?"

"Yes," I answer him although it feels like a half-truth and just thinking that I'm partially lying to him makes my pulse quicken and body heat. It's not the same. What I did with Nikolai wasn't anywhere close to this. We were young, and I needed someone to offer me comfort. Nikolai was the only one there for me. I kissed him first, and I begged him to touch me.

I loved him, and I knew he loved me. Even if he would only ever be a friend.

But my father could never know about us and when Nik moved up in the ranks and I grew bolder, my father grew suspicious. I don't think Nikolai ever wanted to risk his position for me.

And I didn't want to risk our friendship.

What I had with him was nothing like this.

"Who was it?" Carter asks me. "More than one?" His head tilts as he releases my hand and my heart beats like a war drum.

"None of your business," I tell him playfully and

grab both of his wrists to move his hands to the armrests of the chair. "Let me play," I tell him as if it's a command, but the words come out as if I'm begging.

He doesn't answer me, but his fingers wrap around the armrests and he doesn't say anything to stop me.

I fumble with the button, my nerves getting the better of me as I move to my knees in between his legs. The sound of his pants rustling and the deep hum of desire from Carter's chest fuel me to ignore my nerves.

He lifts his hips to help me after I unzip his pants and his cock juts out in front of my face. Shock catches me off guard. It's larger than I thought. Veiny and thick. Instantly, I wonder how he fit inside of me. Squirming in front of him, I know he knows what I'm thinking. The rough and masculine chuckle gives it away.

I glance up at him as I wrap his dick with both my hands. I can't possibly close my fingers around him, but the part that worries me is how I'll fit him in my mouth.

I imagined taking all of him and pleasuring him to the point where he couldn't control himself, but now I question if I can take a fraction of him without gagging.

Slowly, Carter lifts his hand as if asking for permission and moves it to the back of my head. "You can lick it first," he offers low and deep, not hiding how his breathing has hitched.

The bead of precum at his slit entices me to lick it, and so I do. A blush and pride rise to heat my cheeks as the man seated in front of me shudders at my touch.

His large hand splays and brings me closer to him, urging me on for more. But I tsk him, grabbing his hand and placing it back where it belongs on the armrest.

He readjusts in his seat, but his eyes never leave mine. They're darker than before, which only makes the silver specks stand out even more. The heat there leaves me wanting and I lean forward, finding my pleasure by covering the head of his cock with my lips.

The salty taste of precum and the feel of Carter's thighs tightening under my forearms as I brace myself, make me moan with my mouth full of him.

"Fuck," he groans, and his hips buck slightly, pushing him further into my mouth, moving against the roof and down my throat. And I take him easily, although my teeth scrape along his dick.

Using my lips to shield my teeth, I put pressure on his cock, taking every inch of him that I can.

My eyes burn as I lower myself more and more, and each time I get hotter and hotter for him. The thought of getting on top of him and taking my pleasure from him crosses my mind, but I resist. I want to show him I can give him pleasure like he gives me.

My nails dig into my thighs as I feel the head of his dick hit the back of my throat. It takes everything I have not to react. To not pull away and gasp for air as he suffocates me when his hips tip up and he shoves himself just a bit past my breaking point.

I sputter slightly, forcing him out of my mouth so I can breathe. I lean back but I don't stop. Even knowing there's saliva around my mouth, I keep working his cock with my hand and quickly take him back in and try to deep throat him again. The deep, gruff groan that Carter unleashes as I hollow my cheeks makes me feel like a queen. Like a powerful queen able to bring this man to his knees.

Through my lashes, I peek at him. At his stiff position and his blunt nails digging into the leather of his chair as he holds onto it instead of reaching out for me. My eyes drift upward as I take him deeper, trying to swallow. And at that moment Carter breaks.

"Enough," he bites out and stands up, pulling his cock from my mouth and leaving me on my ass in front of him. My palms hit the floor hard, but I don't care. The only feeling in my body I care about is the throbbing pulse between my thighs.

I can barely control my breathing as I look up at him. Carter Cross. Unhinged and unable to give up control. "I want you," I plead with him from beneath him.

It's true. I want him, and I'm unwilling to hide that fact any longer.

He turns his back to me, his pants sagging around his waist until he shoves them down, showing me his tight ass and muscular thighs.

His forearm braces against his desk and in one swift motion he clears it all to the floor. The phone, pens, his laptop, the papers. They flutter and crash to the ground all at once, but none of those things matter. The only thing I can do is stay victim to the intensity of Carter's needs.

"I want you to ride my face. I need to feel you cum

on my tongue." His words make the ache between my thighs even greater. My need to feel him come undone even stronger.

My legs feel weak and ready to buckle as I stand, but it doesn't matter. Carter grips my hips and forces a yelp from me as he lies across his desk, his still-hard cock jutting out as he lets me sit on his chest.

Before a single word is spoken in between my gasps for breath, Carter shoves my skirt up and shreds my panties.

As I watch the tattered lingerie fall to the floor, Carter reaches for my blouse, ripping it from the top and exposing my breasts. He tears at my clothes like they're nothing. And they may as well be, judging by how quickly and easily they fall to his whim.

He said he wanted me to ride him. But Carter's a fucking liar. His fingers grip the flesh of my hips and ass and he keeps me right where he wants me. He drags his tongue from my opening up to my clit, where he sucks to the point of me falling forward with a blinding pleasure that lights every nerve ending on fire.

My breasts hit the desk above his head and as I scream out, the door to the office opens.

I cover myself and try to hide, but Carter's still ravaging my pussy when I catch Daniel's shocked expression.

"Fuck," is all he says, and he turns as quickly as he can to leave, reaching behind him for the doorknob but failing to grab it. I'd laugh if I wasn't petrified, knowing I'm about to cum. The pleasure swirls into a storm in my belly and threatens to ride through every limb, moving to the tips of my fingers in waves.

"I'm going to cum," I cry out to the ceiling as Carter lifts me off him, shoving me down against his hard cock where it brushes against my ass, so he can see who the hell opened the door.

The door slams shut finally, and Carter sits up, making me fall back against the desk while his thick cock runs along the length of my pussy and I cum. The feel of his cock just barely brushing up against my entrance is what does it.

I cum violently, with my face and every inch of my body heated. I can hear Carter grabbing his pants and pulling them up his legs even as the pleasure rolls through me, paralyzing me and heating my body all at once.

Daniel Cross, brother to the most powerful man I've ever met, just witnessed me riding Carter's face and taking my pleasure from him.

I shudder as my hand reaches up to cover my breasts. I can barely breathe as I hear Carter pull up his zipper.

I should feel shame of some sort. But I can't bring myself to do it. I feel nothing but sated, breathless and fulfilled.

"I have to see what Daniel needs. Leave one heel on each side of the desk," Carter commands me while grabbing each of my ankles and spreading my legs apart on his desk. "Wait for me."

He grips my hips, pulling me closer to the edge of

the desk as I nod. My skirt is rumpled around me and my hands instantly move to my pussy.

"If you want to touch yourself, do it." His command comes in between his ragged breaths. "Cum as much as you want while I'm gone."

I lie there, my back on his desk, my ass directed to the seat he rules in and my chest heaving as he leaves me.

I'm still catching my breath when I hear the door close.

Touch yourself, I hear his words again and moan just from the command. From the deep voice and cadence that can only come from a man's voice filled with desire.

My fingers trail over my clit, but I can't do it.

I'm so sensitive to even the slightest touch that I have to stop my movements before pushing myself over. I can't do it. It's so intense, I simply can't bring myself to the edge.

I clench around nothing, I picture Carter between my legs, on top of me, smothering me with his weight as he pounds into me and I have to scissor my legs. My hands fly to my hair, pushing it from my face and trying to get a grip.

When I open my eyes, I stare at the blank ceiling, accompanied only by my heavy breathing and the ticking of the clock.

It doesn't stop ticking, but with each stroke, my needs diminish, and my sanity comes back to me.

I lie there for what feels like hours, and when I check the clock, it's accurate. Over an hour has passed, my back is stiff and the desire I had is all but gone, subdued by concern, replaced with a feeling of rejection. As I sit up, everything hurts. My back, especially. I stare at the door, willing Carter to come to get me. But he doesn't come back.

Not this hour and not the next.

Any bit of power I felt, fades to nothing, which is exactly what I feel like when I slink out of the room, covering myself with the torn shirt.

I HAVEN'T STOPPED STARING at the clock in the bedroom and wondering if I should go back to the office. I can't possibly lie there waiting for him for hours. I'm almost certain he didn't expect that when he left me.

But every minute that passes warns me to go back. To stop defying Carter and show him that I can be what he wants, and maybe that would convince him to do what I want. To spare my family.

The pride and thrill are long gone and in their place only uncertainty.

All I'm doing is worrying as I restlessly wait in Carter's bed.

The moment I hear the click of the door opening, I sit up straight in bed, getting on my knees, clutching the sheets to my chest.

Carter walks in slowly, his gaze on the floor. He looks exhausted and beat down like I've never seen him. I can't get a word out, shocked by the sight of him in this state, but the excuses I've drummed up and rehearsed in the last few hours don't matter anyway.

He apologizes. Carter apologizes to me for the second time in only a matter of two days.

"I'm sorry I kept you waiting this long. I didn't realize..." his voice trails off as he heads to the dresser, carelessly dropping his Rolex into a drawer and then taking his time to strip down.

The muscles in his shoulders ripple as he undresses with his back to me.

"Is everything okay?" I ask him, daring to pry.

His five o'clock shadow is thick, and his eyes look heavy. It's only then that I wonder if he slept at all last night.

I barely sleep as it is, and Carter's always awake when I drift off and always out of bed when I wake up.

"Daniel isn't in a good place at the moment," he tells me in a single drawn-out breath before climbing into bed.

"Problems with Addison?" I can only guess.

Carter's gaze turns curious, but also guarded as he watches me scoot closer to him. I wonder how much of this is an act, and how much of this is really my desire to get closer to Carter as I let my hand fall to his chest. It's awkward at first for me to lay my cheek on his bare chest while my fingers play with the smattering of chest hair that leads lower and lower. But the more he allows it, the more he wraps his arm around me like I belong there, the more comfortable I feel taking what I want from him.

"What do you know about her?" he asks me, and I feel the words rumble from his chest.

"Just that she's with Daniel," I tell him and then remember the first time I saw her. How upset both of them were over something I wasn't privy to. I add quietly, "I think they love each other."

I don't have to look up to know that Carter's smiling, but I do. But the small smile is weak; the bleakness can't be hidden even by Carter's handsome lips.

"She's not handling lockdown well," he confides in me. Lockdown. I've heard the term more than once. I know what it means, and it reminds me of the reality. My father would often leave me in the safe house for days at a time if he had to leave during lockdown. It was better when he would only be gone for hours and I could hide in my room, which I did regardless of whether we were on lockdown or not.

The words are barely spoken as my chest tightens. "I can imagine."

"You stayed in your cell for longer than I thought you would without submitting to me. You have a mental strength that most don't." I don't know how to take Carter's statement. It's not a compliment, although it feels like it.

"Still, I can see her wanting to leave. To not be..." I try to think of the right word, a word that won't upset Carter and ruin the conversation. My fingers weave around the thin chain ever present around my neck. The expensive necklace that's truly a collar.

"Tethered?" Carter questions and I can only nod,

my cheek brushing against his chest as I stare straight ahead.

The silence lasts longer than I'd like it to, but all I can do is listen to the steady rhythm of Carter's heart until he speaks.

"She's safe here. She's cared for." The way he says his words is careful, yet tense. That, combined with the way his heart picks up its pace, makes me think we're not talking about Addison anymore.

"What would you tell her then?" I ask him, wanting an insight into Carter's thoughts. "The moment she's alone and the thoughts of leaving race back to her?" I have to know what he would say. "What would you tell her?"

Carter moves for the first time since I've settled next to him. He lifts the arm wrapped around me and lets his fingers slowly trail along my skin as if he's carefully considering his answer. He kisses my hair once, then twice before using his other hand to lift up my chin and force me to look at him. His touch is gentle. So gentle it could break me.

"I'd tell her she has someone here who loved her before she even knew the darkest levels to where love can take you. And that there's no better protection from the shit life we lead than that."

My heart stops. I feel it cease to beat as he continues to stare at me, and I can't will it to move again. There's nothing but sincerity in his gaze and the last bit of guard I have crumbles.

Love. The word love breaks something deep inside of me.

"I need this one for me," Carter says before I can respond. He rolls over, pinning me beneath him and fucks me roughly, kisses me ravenously and then holds me to him, my back to his chest. All the while I break more and more. So much so, that I know I'll never be the same again.

CHAPTER 10

Carter

"What's the update?" I ask Jase, leaning against the wall in the hall. My eyes stay pinned on the carved glass doorknob with my thoughts on what's behind it.

"Same as before." Jase's answer comes out low as we both see Aria and Daniel making their way toward us. They're far enough away that she won't be able to hear. Her fingers twist around one another as she walks quickly to keep up with Daniel's pace.

I don't know what Daniel tells her with a wide grin, but it cracks the solemn look on her face and she smiles back at him.

"Romano's ready to strike when we are. As far as everyone knows, it's the two of us taking out Talvery."

"And the drug? What about the buyers hoarding it?"

"They're all saying Marcus. But it's only a name." I know what he's getting at. When a man is close to death, he'll tell you anything you want to know, either to make his ending quick or to try to save himself. Four men now, each hoarding the drug we know to be lethal and each only giving up a single name in their last breath. Those are the only four buying in bulk, except for the girl I saw a week ago. I'd rather not seek her out, but our options are dwindling.

"Why not give more information?"

Jase's palm presses against the wall and I can feel his gaze on me as he leans closer. "What does he have on them that they keep his secrets even as they die?"

"Maybe they don't know anything else," I offer, but Jase shakes his head. I only glance up at him because of Aria. She sees his expression and the bit of happiness Daniel provided her instantly vanishes.

Jase looks worried, angry even with a scowl plastered across his face.

"We'll talk about it later," I tell him lowly, but he doesn't stop.

"They didn't give me anything. Not a drop-off point, not a procedure or any details at all." He leans in closer to me to emphasize, "Only a name."

Our gazes are locked for a moment longer than they should be.

Daniel clears his throat at the same time that I hear his and Aria's footsteps come to a stop behind me.

"Then we have a name," I tell Jase and a small twitch gathers on the corner of his lips.

"Later," I remind him. "We'll talk later." He nods, pushing off the wall and finally nodding a hello to Aria.

"I hope you like it," Jase tells her, and she glances between the two of us, not knowing what the hell he's talking about.

As Daniel and Jase walk away, heading back the way Daniel and Aria came, she tells him, *thank you*, to which she's given a smile from both of my brothers.

Her nervousness is still visible as she barely glances toward me and continues to run her fingers along the seam of her blouse. Anything out of the normal routine causes this reaction in her.

I wonder how long that will last.

The drunken comment she made the other night hasn't left me. That night, as soon as she was asleep, I made arrangements.

She said she's going to leave me one day. That she's going to run away and hide in her room until the war is done with. She was drunk, but she said it as if it was a fact.

She doesn't remember saying it, but that doesn't change anything.

I won't let her leave me. She's never allowed to leave me.

I asked her why she'd leave me, and she said so simply, that sometimes she just wants to breathe but can't even do that without overthinking everything.

I won't give her a bedroom, but she can have a room to run to.

I can hide what's going on from her until her questions fade and all she has left is me.

"What is this?" Aria asks as the door opens.

"It was a storage room," I answer her with one hand splayed on her lower back and one hand on the door to push it open as far as it'll go.

"And now?" she asks aimlessly as she takes a step into the brightly lit room. Her face is filled with awe as she steps further into the lushly decorated room.

Other than a gray paisley wallpapered wall to the left, where one would presume a bed to sit, the remainder of the walls are a soft blush, nearly white.

The chair at the vanity is lined with a matching gray striped fabric and beyond it are glass vases and a matching glass standing light.

Gray and blush are the only two colors. The decorator referred to the color scheme as mineral tones, but it looks feminine as fuck to me. I wanted Aria to know this room was designed for her, so every piece of furniture and item contained in this room was meant to ensure she knew it belonged to her.

Everything else, from the plush white rug in the center of the room to the sheer curtains, is white. A glass table and mirrored nightstands allow the light to shine through with no obstructions.

It didn't take long for the company to put it together. Her room is at the other end of my wing, farthest away from my bedroom. It was Jase's suggestion and the only reason I agreed was due to my impatience. I needed it done quickly considering we're only days away from all-out war.

"What do you want in return?" Aria asks me hesitantly.

My expression turns hard for a moment while I consider her. "This isn't a negotiation or a game, Aria. It's a gift." Her beautiful hazel eyes widen slightly and her lips part to apologize, but I interrupt her to ask, "Do you like it?"

"It's beautiful," she says reverently as she admires the details of each of the pieces, only taking small glances at me to keep track of how I'm assessing her as she reacts to the room.

"There's no bed?" she asks quietly with a touch of confusion as she stares toward the wall where one should obviously sit.

"You can sleep in my room..." I almost add, "or the cell," but I choose not to. She seems to hear the words regardless, her eyes drifting to the floor as she swallows thickly.

"This isn't a room I'd like you to consider your bedroom." My words bring her gaze back to me. Choosing my words carefully, I tell her, "You belong with me, but this is a place for you to go if you need... space."

She only nods, and I think that's all the reaction I'll get until she peeks up at me, her fingers trailing along the patterned wallpaper, and says softly, "Thank you." The gratitude melts the tension between us, and it soothes a deep need inside of me for her to want what I can give her.

I watch Aria walk hesitantly to the vanity, intricately carved and an antique, but stunning. She barely touches the cut glass knobs before pulling out the drawers and finding her things there.

Not the ones she had at her home, but new ones to replace each item she had.

Her hand hovers above them for a moment, almost as if she's afraid she'll be bitten by something inside if she moves too quickly.

Her pace is quicker as she moves to the closet, filled with all kinds of clothing. From expensive dresses and lingerie to nightshirts I was told she prefers.

"I enjoy picking out what you wear," I tell her and catch her attention as she turns to look at me, although her hand is still caressing the silk of a deep red blouse.

"And you choose red," she says beneath her breath before turning back to the closet. "There's certainly a theme."

"Red complements you well," I answer her although she doesn't respond. I take a single step toward her, but she continues to examine the room, taking in each bit with care.

"If you'd like something changed," I tell her as she opens a nightstand drawer, "it can be arranged."

She stares at me as she shuts the drawer. There's an edge to her movements.

"How did you know?" she asks, and her question is laced with tension.

"Know what, exactly?" I ask her, my muscles coiling from the tone of her voice.

Her gaze shifts to the open door before her eyes land on me. Her fingers play with the edge of her blouse in a nervous fidget.

"You have a lot of things here." She licks her lip and debates on continuing, but she doesn't need to.

"I asked for a list," I answer her before she can ask how I knew what she'd want.

"There's a rat," she whispers, and her posture turns stiff.

"How did you think Romano knew when and where to acquire you?"

"Acquire... is that what you call it?" Her voice rises as she stalks toward me. Slow, deliberate steps and I can feel the tension rolling off of her shoulders. "The rat told you where to acquire your whore and what to fill her room with?" she asks me with shaky breaths and tears in her eyes.

"I wanted this to be nice for you." The hard words linger between us as my throat tightens. Anger is written on my face; I can feel it like stone, but I can't change my expression.

Of every smart comment and tiny bit of anger she's shown me, this is the worst.

Distrust is clearly evident. I didn't earn her distrust. I'm not the fucking rat.

"How did you expect me to react to being told someone was spying on me?" she asks with genuine distress as her lower lip wobbles and she catches it between her teeth before turning her back to me. I thought she already knew. She's a smart woman, but I forget how trusting she is. How loyal.

Her arms cross and uncross as she debates on how to handle the revelation. She paces from the dresser to the vanity. Already pacing in this room. I have to fight the urge to smirk as I watch her pace back and forth over the white rug, which is exactly how I pictured her in here.

But not so soon, and not like this. This room is better than the cell if nothing else.

"I thought you would have assumed," I tell her honestly and nervousness prickles my skin as she glares back at me. It's unsettling and I debate on leaving her here, but I refuse. She's not going to take her anger out on me. Not when it belongs to someone else. "It wasn't supposed to upset you. I wanted you to have everything you could have possibly wanted," I admit to her and try to keep my voice even and calm, but the anger toward her response still lingers.

The nervousness grows inside of me, and I'm sickened by it. I thought she would appreciate this. I thought she would be excited to have everything she had before. Or at least grateful. I thought wrong.

I should feel irritated or pissed, but that's not what I feel at all. I've done this to her. She can't accept a gift without being cautious of my intentions.

With a growing pit in my stomach, I speak without meeting her eyes. I stare straight ahead at the hanging curtains that are only meant to add beauty to the locked windows that will never open for her.

"I wanted to make you happy," I tell her and clear my throat of the spiked knot. "I thought this would make you happy," I pause to run my hand over the back of my head, feeling the ever-present crease that reminds me how shitty I am at knowing what she needs beyond a good fuck and finally look into her thoughtful gaze that's already softening, "or at least provide you comfort."

My heart beats faster as she stares back at me with a kindness she hasn't before given me. "I'm trying to be gentle," I confess to her.

"I'm sorry," she whispers in a choked voice. The second I feel myself wavering and losing the man I am to this woman, she wanders toward me and wraps her arms around my waist, her hands splaying on my shoulders as she hugs me.

It takes me a moment to hold her to me and when I do, I kiss her hair and bury my face in it before she pulls away.

Her eyes are glassy but she doesn't cry; she sounds strong, although a few of her words crack as she says, "It's just a reminder… of everything that I'll never have again." She gestures to the room and exhales deeply before adding, "It's beautiful and it does give me comfort. You have no idea how much I love this. I do." She swallows with her eyes closed and then runs her fingers through her hair. I wait patiently for her to continue.

"I'm sorry, it's just… there's always something that happens that proves I know nothing and I'm lost."

"You're not lost." My response is immediate, and my tone is one I expect from myself. It's not to be questioned. "You belong here, with me."

Her shoulders steady as her breathing calms and her formerly emotionally-distraught features calm once again, but it's an act. She's brimming inside with a mixture of fear, betrayal, anger, and confusion.

"You're only lost because you want to be," I tell her low and deep, reaching out and pulling her small body closer to me.

Her hands land on my chest and she gasps slightly before looking up at me.

"I can give you everything. I can give you what you never even dreamed of before." I mean every word. I can and will.

Her long hair shines in the light as she nods, making it swish along her collarbone. She's compliant, but her wide eyes are full of questions. Questions she doesn't ask me. Some of them I'm grateful I won't have to answer.

"If you want to run, you run here."

"Carter, there are things you can't replace." She looks straight ahead at my chest as she speaks and her shoulders shudder. "Money can't replace--"

"I'm fully aware of what money can't replace. Nothing can erase the past. Nothing can bring it back." The sharp edge of my words and the pain and anger I refuse to hide in them erase her desperation to beg me for what I will never give her.

"I'll give you what I can. Everything that I'm able. But sometimes what we want most is impossible to achieve." My throat tightens with emotion and just as it does, Aria props herself up on her tiptoes, gently caresses my face and kisses me.

It's short and only a peck. Only a small kiss. Nothing like what we've shared before.

It feels different than it has before. Her touch is hesitant. A different kind of fear is in control of her and shows in her eyes. The kiss is meant to put an end to the conversation. She's hiding in that act.

"Tell me what you're thinking," I command her although the edge of desperation is evident to me. I don't think she can hear it. I pray she can't.

Her answer doesn't come quickly. She tries to leave me, and I cling to her, but she grabs my wrists and pulls my touch away as she tells me, "I'm scared."

"You don't have anything to fear if you obey me," I tell her, pinning her gaze to mine.

"You don't understand," she whispers.

The unspoken words between us are causing a crack in the delicate balance of what we have.

The reality that she's still my prisoner.

The truth that I won't rest until her father is dead.

The fact that she won't forgive me for killing everyone she's ever known and loved.

And the fact I never want to be without her and I think she feels the same about me. If only she could accept what's to come.

The Talverys will be massacred. And she, the sole survivor of her name, belongs to me.

CHAPTER 11

Aria

IT'S TOO MUCH, I think with my thumbnail in between my teeth as I lie in the soaking tub.

Every day, something changes, and I never know how to react or what it means for us. What it means about me.

How could I not have known someone was watching me?

It must have been Mika.

He was always watching and taunting and teasing, but I thought it was just because he was an asshole on a power trip.

I lower my hand back into the steaming water and try to settle against the edge of the tub. My foot slips up to the faucet, feeling the hot water splash against it.

I can feel my fight leaving. The urge to keep fighting and keep holding on to the girl I was before Carter *acquired* me is trickling out of me day by day.

He's going to kill my family. My father. Nikolai. I know Carter will, no matter how much he cares for me.

That's the most painful part. I think he does care for me, but Carter is ruthless and there's nothing I can do to stop him. There's no point in trying.

The hopelessness presses against my shoulders, threatening to push me under and drown away my sorrows.

I wish I was numb to it all. There's nothing worse than being fully aware yet having no way to change any of it. Without fighting, I feel like a traitor. I'm not just surviving anymore. I'm living, and I don't know how I can forgive myself for having feelings for the man who's responsible for so many horrible sins.

Just as I feel tears pricking at my eyes, Carter's voice startles me. "You're tense."

I try to hide my sniffling and feel pathetic that I'm crying at all. Carter ignores it though, offering me that small bit of mercy as he strips down and slowly sinks into the tub, scooting me forward so he can lie in the bath behind me. The water sloshes and rises higher up my body as he sinks into the tub.

His touch is gentle, and I don't fail to notice that he's hard already. Just the thought of his cock makes my thighs clench and the dull ache that never leaves sends a wave of want through me.

Maybe that's why I don't want to fight him. The

only thing that takes away the pain and anger is the one thing he gives me constantly. And that makes me a whore of the worst kind.

The water sways and a shiver runs down my spine as Carter's large hands press against my shoulders, pulling me into his chest. His fingers drift down my body, over the pearls and diamonds of his necklace that I always wear because he told me to, and the faint touch hardens my nipples and leaves goosebumps in his path to the hot water.

"What are you thinking?" Carter's deep voice rumbles just as I close my eyes and I open them to stare at the tiled wall and answer bluntly.

"I was thinking I don't want to kill you anymore because you fuck me so often." The truth spills out easily, not even questioning my answer to him.

His rough chuckle almost makes me smile as he reaches for the sponge and then dips it into the steaming water.

"I'm so tired," I say absently as Carter runs the sponge along my shoulder and down my forearm.

"It's late. Later than you usually stay awake." I spent hours in the gilded room. That's what I'm calling it now. That's all it is. Even if it is beautiful, and I do love that he had it built for me and I'm grateful to have my things back... or replicas of them.

"When do you even sleep?" I ask him. "You're always awake when I go to sleep, and awake when I wake up."

"I don't like to sleep," he answers me. "I can sleep when I'm dead."

His even tone and lack of humor make my heart tense. Like it doesn't want to beat when he talks like that.

Readjusting, I watch the film of bath oils move on the surface of the water and nestle my foot under Carter's calf.

"You know we could have started this way," I say weakly, not sure if I should broach the subject, but what do I have to lose?

"What way?"

"With you giving me a room and being less of a monster." The words slip out easily and Carter's ministrations pause at the last word. But then he keeps going, continuing to wash me.

"And what would you have done? Destroyed the room and used the shards of glass to kill me?"

He's not wrong. I could easily see that happening and the reality makes the small hairs on the back of my neck stand up.

What happened to that fight? To that edge I'm fully aware would have come out had the situation been different.

Nothing has changed. Carter stole me, keeps me prisoner and he's going to kill my family.

None of that has changed. Yet here I lie against him, loving his touch and finding my heart being ripped into two.

"We should talk about something else," Carter suggests.

The sound of the water falling from my shoulder to the tub is calming. Which is anything but what I should be feeling. The sponge is still hot, and it soothes my tired muscles.

"I could fall asleep in here," I murmur absently. All I want to do anymore is sleep. I don't know if I'm depressed, worn out, or if that's what happens when you lose your fight.

"Can I wash you?" I ask him, wondering if he'd let me.

A moment passes and then he dips the sponge back under; I expect him to give it to me, but that's not what happens.

"I like washing you," he whispers against my ear, his warm breath creating a wave of want that flows through me. But my eyes stay open.

Of course, he wouldn't want me to wash him. He couldn't even let me suck his dick. A small huff of feigned humor leaves me, and I readjust in the water so that the sound of it splashing will drown out the huff, but he hears it anyway.

"What?" he asks and leans forward to look at my expression, pulling my shoulder against his to keep me from avoiding him.

I meet his dark gaze, the grays and silvers seeming to take over in the bathroom light. "Nothing, it just feels good. It's nice to feel cared for."

Without speaking he leans back, kisses the crook of my neck, and moves the sponge to my neck and chest.

"Did you think it would be this way from the beginning?" I ask him. Truly wanting to know what he thought back then, only weeks ago. The reminder of the cell, of me starving and dying of both boredom and fear should make me angry, but all it does is make me pity Carter.

"I didn't know what to expect from you. I only knew I wanted to have you."

"To have me," I echo and settle my head in the crook of his neck. The movement makes my breasts rise above the surface of the water for a moment and the chill is unwelcome until I settle back into the water.

"Your choice of words always seems to amaze me." My voice is flat, and I wish I could take it back. Silence stretches, and I wonder how long I've been in the water.

You can't wash everything away, but I wish I could.

"How did you think this would end?"

"You're asking a lot of questions tonight," he says instead of giving me an answer and places the sponge back on its shelf rather than answering me.

"Oh, and I see I've found the question that crosses the line," I tell him with a smile although a deep pain courses through my heart as I shut my eyes. Each beat feeling harder and taking more of me just to keep going. I can only imagine what Carter wanted to do with me.

"It all changed when I saw how much you wanted me. When I saw how much you craved my touch... how much you needed me." I open my eyes as Carter's fingers reach for my chin, the water dripping into the tub as he forces me to look into his eyes.

"I need you to want me still when this is over." Carter's words hold an edge of sincerity that's too much to handle.

I almost ask why, but I'm afraid of the answer I'll get. I'm afraid what I feel for him isn't reciprocated. I've been foolish before, and I'm almost certain I am now.

"I'm not afraid of you," I confess to him, wanting to at least hint at the depths of what I feel for him.

"You should be." He doesn't try to make his words gentle in the least. "You need to be."

In his presence, my body turns to fire. He ignites something inside of me like no one else ever has. I doubt anyone else could ever affect me the way he does. Some moments, I hate him and who he is, and what he's done and will do. But unless those thoughts are on the forefront of my mind, the hate fades and it's replaced with a lust that clouds my judgment and demands my body bow to his. To show him love like he's never seen and the power of what it can do to heal him.

What's more? I crave it more every day. I'm addicted to Carter Cross. And the shame of that fact, although present, has quieted.

But the voice is still there and picks away at me. It's relentless, but so is Carter.

CHAPTER 12

Carter

SOME MOMENTS, I feel closer to her.

Others, more distant.

I wish I knew what to make of her tonight. Nothing went as I thought it would and that puts me on edge.

She fell asleep in the tub, and as I carry her small form wrapped in a towel to bed, I can't help but notice how peaceful she looks.

Tonight, was like knowing you're in the eye of a storm. She's calm and placated but beneath the surface, everything she's truly feeling rage inside of her. She needs to let it go.

I have to set her down and pull the comforter from underneath her before she can bury herself into the mattress.

As she nestles into the sheets, she wakes calmly.

Rubbing her eyes, she comes to and asks, "Is it morning?" She practically hums the words.

With her damp hair a mess and sleep lingering in her expression, she's fucking gorgeous.

I cup her cheek and plant a soft kiss on her lips, to which she lifts hers up and deepens it. I'm growing addicted to the way she kisses me. How she doesn't hide her passion in her touch.

Unlike in her gifted room today. I want them all to be like this one.

I've never kissed a woman before her. Never let myself fall for anyone or given them that part of me. So, every peck, every time she deepens it, it means so much more than I thought it would. I need more of *this* from her.

"Not yet, songbird." Whispering against her lips I tell her, "You fell asleep in the bath."

She slowly sits up as I climb into bed next to her.

"Well, I don't feel tired now," she tells me and sits cross-legged.

Exhaustion sweeps over me as I lie down and pull her close to me. "Good, I can have you then," I tell her, letting my lips drag against her neck to leave a trail of open-mouth kisses. I rock my erection into her hip and then pin her under me. "I wanted you in the bath."

I'd planned on putting one heel on each side of the tub, just as I'd told her to do in the office, but her questions were more important. More insightful, even though I didn't like where they were going.

126

It feels like she's slipping from me, slowly. I'm losing her, and I don't know how or why.

But I'll get her back. She has nowhere else to run and no one else.

She only needs to accept that.

Her hand sweeps behind my neck and she pulls my lips to hers, taking and demanding. "Make me forget," she whispers against my lips and my chest aches at her words.

I need to forget, just as she does. It's so easy to get lost in her.

My fingers trail down the dip in her waist slowly until I find her cunt. Already hot and wet and needy, she rocks herself into my palm and I smile against her lips.

Nipping her lower lip and guiding my cock to her entrance, I tease her, "You're always ready for me."

"Always," she mewls just before I slam into her to the hilt.

"Fuck!" she yells out as I pull out and then thrust into her slowly, taken aback at the tone of her strangled cry.

Her palms press against my chest, pushing me away as I kiss the crook of her neck and she moans a painful sound. "Carter," she whispers my name with agony. Her brow is etched with a look of pain.

"It hurts," she gasps, arching her neck as I pull out of her completely. "It hurts," she repeats, trying to close her legs. Shit. My body tenses concerned that I hurt her. Fuck. Not like this.

"Shh," I whisper against her neck and kiss her

lightly as my fingers find her clit. She needs to feel good under me. I can't have her any other way.

Instantly, she moans that sweet sound of pleasure I love hearing. "I was wondering how much I could fuck you before you'd be too sore." She only replies with a quick inhale and the buck of her hips which does nothing but give me slight relief.

"Look at me," I command her, and her head turns instantly to face me. Her gorgeous hazel-green eyes burn into mine. My thumb rubs ruthless circles around her clit and Aria bites into her lower lip, desperate to keep her eyes on me but knowing the pleasure will rock through her soon.

Her back bows slightly and her breaths turns to pants, but instead of letting her get off, I lower my fingers, trailing them through her lips and gathering the wetness to bring it lower.

"I could always take you here," I say lowly, pressing my fingers against her forbidden entrance.

Aria's answer is to open her mouth wider with a look of shock, but more than that, sinful curiosity.

A smile stretches across my lips as I say, "Not tonight though. I have to play with you first." Her eyes light again with curiosity and the guilt I felt a moment ago diminishes. I bring my fingers back to her clit then down to her entrance, pressing them inside her gently, but even that makes her wince.

I have to pull the covers back to look at her slick folds; she's red and swollen, well used.

That doesn't mean I can't give her pleasure and that I can't have mine in return. If I've learned anything about Aria, it's that the more I give her pleasure, the more compliant she is.

Her eyes stay pinned on me as she looks down her body and waits for what I'll do to her.

I run my tongue up and down her pussy and then suck on her clit. She's so fucking sweet. The taste of her on my lips makes my cock twitch with need. With her hands in my hair and her heels digging into the bed she finds her release, screaming out my name.

She curls on her side as I move back up the bed and lie next to her, not waiting to position her just as I want her. With one hand on her breast and the other pushing the hair away from her flushed face, she's still reeling from her orgasm when I move my cock between her thighs.

"Arch your back," I tell her, and she obeys instantly, jutting her ass out. And it tempts me. The curve of her waist and the round flesh of her ass are so seductive. I can just imagine gripping on to her and rocking into her as she screams in ecstasy.

She's not ready for my dick to take her ass though… not yet.

I settle on pushing the head of my cock inside her, only the head and wait for her reaction. A small moan escapes her lips as she rocks gently, finding the after-shocks pleasurable. I know there will be a bite of pain, but there's nothing better than when pain and pleasure mix.

"Grab my cock," I give her the command, and she reaches around to take my cock and stroke it. "Harder," I say then put my hand over hers and show her how to jerk me off. She only has a grip on the base of my dick, but her unsure hold and the lust in her eyes are enough to get me off. Even without her pussy clenching around the head of my cock.

"Fuck," I groan as she rubs me and slowly pushes more of me inside of her. With my hand on her hip, I stop her from pushing more of me inside of her. Even with her getting off, it'll only make her worse off and all I need is this.

"I want you every night, however I can have you." My words are tense as I sit on the edge of my release.

The air between us is different now. There's a raw quality neither of us can hide, although I'll never admit it.

Her pressure is firm, her strokes even and deliberate, and then her pussy spasms around the tip of my dick as she cums again from me rubbing her clit.

But it's the way she's looking at me that gets me off. Like I'm hers to play with. I'm hers to fuck, to use.

Like she owns me, as she strokes my dick and I cum inside her.

My eyes beg me to close them as I revel in the sweet burst of satisfaction and I mark her again. But her gaze stays on mine, our breath mingling, and I'm forced to get lost in her hazel eyes. I'm still cumming when she releases me, turning and kissing me hard, crashing her lips to mine and devouring me.

My cum leaks from her and onto the sheets, but she doesn't care and neither do I.

Her heart races as she presses her breasts to my chest and belly to mine. Once again wanting to get closer to me, and I feel for the first time today I have her back. She's mine again.

The day I stop fucking her will be the day I lose her. She needs my touch like I need the air she breathes.

"I think I might be able to sleep now," she whispers and then smiles against my lips.

"Sleep well." I keep my voice calm and soothing, rubbing my arm up and down her bare back as she settles her head on my chest, a new habit of hers. One I approve of.

Looking up at me with her head resting on my arm she tells me, "Sweet dreams."

I kiss her gently as she drifts off to sleep in my arms with the faint taste of lust still on her lips.

ADDICTS WILL GET *high on anything*. My father's words ring in my ears. The white lights are too bright. I wince.

Where am I? My head lolls to the side; it's so heavy I can't lift it. *Everything hurts.*

Slowly, I feel each of my limbs. My wrists won't move, pinned against a metal chair. The same with my ankles and every inch of me is in pain, but the worst is radiating from my stomach.

I heave up a breath that squeezes my chest, coughing up blood.

Fuck.

My right eye is swollen, and I try to open it,

remembering how my mother's pills fell into the gutter. No, we needed that money.

My father said the addicts would buy them, but hardly any of them did. I stayed out all day, and only two buyers paid me anything. And then the men showed up. Talvery's men.

"How long was he there?"

I hear someone from across the room ask the question and open my eyes to see a swinging light and a man in a crisp suit with long black hair slicked back tossing my wallet across a metal table littered with tools.

A groan tears from me as I try to move. Try to get away. I know he's going to kill me. I know it.

But it's hopeless.

"I'm sorry," I spew and more blood spits up. "I didn't know," I try to say but my throat is so dry and feels bruised. I don't think they heard me, so I repeat myself, pleading for mercy. "I didn't know."

"You didn't know what, kid?" a man hisses in front of me. Pain spikes at the back of my scalp as he grips my hair and shakes my head to look at him. "You didn't know you were dealing on my turf?" His eyes are a pale blue and ice cold. "The whole east side knows it now. So, you're fucked." He spits out the words then leaves me, picking up something from the metal table.

Every crunch of bone, every rip of my skin, every deep gouge pushes me closer and closer until I'm holding on to life by a thread.

I even cry out for my mother.

They all laugh in the room. But still, I cry out for

her. Praying she can't see this and what's happened only weeks after her death. Shame and regret and pain make my head feel light and slowly I feel weightless. So close to death.

Please, just end it. I don't want to live anymore. I can't.

Bang. Bang. Bang.

At first, I think they're guns that wake me, stopping me from drifting to lifelessness.

Bang. Another bang at the door so close to me, yet impossible to reach.

"Please, I need you," someone says, and her voice sends a chill through my body, but at the same time, warmth. "I need you." The words are feminine and soft, but with a plea that begs me to listen.

She needs me.

The pain is still vivid with every move of my limbs, but I can hear her if I listen.

The voice turns harder, colder and the air goes frigid.

"I need you, Carter," she says again but this time there's no negotiation in her tone. "I need you!" she yells at me.

The anger rising and a storm brewing around me, she screams at me, her voice reverberating in the room, "I still need you!"

CHAPTER 13

Aria

His arm feels so heavy. I can barely hear my groan as I wake up and try to push away Carter's arm.

I struggle, but he only squeezes tighter.

My shoulders twist and I push against his arm, but the muscles are coiled, and his grip is too much. I can't breathe.

My eyes shoot open, realizing this isn't a dream.

"Carter!" I cry out in a strangled breath, fighting his hold and letting the anxiety rush through my blood to make me kick backward, shoving and heaving to get him off of me. "Wake up!" My heart pounds harder.

I struggle to breathe. My voice croaks and my lungs burn as I yell, "Carter!"

My chest flies forward as he jolts awake, instantly

releasing me and leaving me breathless and crumpled on the bed. The mattress dips and groans as Carter gets up. I push the hair from my face and then try to steady my ragged breathing.

It was only a moment – a small moment – maybe a minute in time, but I thought he was going to kill me, he held me so tight.

"You scared the shit out of me." I barely get the words out, my eyes still burning.

Without an answer, I turn to him and it's then I see he's breathing just as heavily as I am. With both palms against the wall, he leans over and tries to calm himself down.

My blood runs cold at the sight of him. "Carter?" My voice carries across the room to him, ignoring how my muscles are screaming still from fighting against his grip.

Getting onto my knees, I crawl to the edge of the mattress. His shoulders are tense, and he won't look at me.

Cautiously, I climb off the bed and go to him. "It's okay." I try to keep my voice soothing, but my body hasn't caught up to the fact that he needs me. "I'm okay," I say, trying to reassure him.

With my heart hammering, I gently place a hand on his arm but he's quick to rip it away and stalk to the bathroom, leaving me with a pounding fear racing through my blood.

"Carter," I say hesitantly, but he doesn't respond to me at all.

The question is clear in my mind, go to him or let

him be? I'm still catching my breath and waking up as I push my hair from my hot face, registering what just happened.

If I've ever seen a man who shouldn't be left alone, it's Carter. He's too broken, and there's no telling what he'll do.

"Was it just a nightmare?" I ask him innocently, wanting him to give me anything. I can feel the rug end and the wood begin as I walk toward him in the dark.

He flicks on the light in the bathroom and runs the water. And I walk toward the sound and strip of light from the bathroom that guides me.

"Carter?" I ask him softly as I push the bathroom door open and see his back to me again. His muscles ripple as he washes his face.

"Please, talk to me," I whisper weakly when he still doesn't answer me. Even after he's dried off his face. "Are you okay?"

I can see him swallow in the mirror. I can see the weary expression of a man who's led a horrible life. The fatigue in his eyes. The pain etched in the faint scars on his back.

He presses his palms to his eyes and breathes in and out. "Go to bed," he commands in a harsh tone I don't expect, although, I don't leave as asked.

My heart squeezes with pain. I won't leave him like this. "I don't want to," I tell him with barely any courage, the words coming out shaky.

"What happened?" I ask him in a comforting whisper. "It was just a dream," I tell him, hoping they'll have more comfort for him than those words do for me.

For the first time, he looks at me in the mirror, and the sight of him sends a chill down my spine. The power, the anger, the man who rules and gives no mercy expecting none in return, pierces me with his gaze.

"Don't tell anyone." His words are soft and they hang in the air with a threat. An unneeded and ridiculous threat.

"Tell anyone what?" I question his sanity at this moment, only to realize he doesn't want me to tell anyone that he had a nightmare. "I wouldn't. I would never." My words come out quickly as tears prick my eyes. "That's not why I'm here, Carter."

"Go to bed," he tells me again, although this time his words are softer.

"Are you okay?" I ask him, taking another small step toward him, but still not sure if I should touch him. All I want to do is hold him, pull him close to me and tell him it's all right. Just like the way he's held me over the past few weeks. But I don't even know what happened.

With his grip on the edge of the sink and his head lowered, his voice comes out quietly and nearly menacing but more than that, heart-wrenching.

"Look at me, Aria." He speaks to me in the mirror, his eyes bloodshot as they stare back at me. "Look at who I am. Nothing about me is okay."

I stand there shaking, my words and breath caught by the intensity of the man in front of me. Even as he turns off the light, leaving me in darkness as he walks around me, his skin barely grazing mine, I tremble. His pace is ruthless as he leaves me, slamming the door and

I'm left stunned and shaken. More than anything, I'm saddened by everything that just happened and so aware of how alone I am as I cry myself to sleep.

CHAPTER 14

Carter

SOMEHOW, I fucked up.

She's the one who was supposed to change when I gave her the knife.

She's the one who should need me.

Not the other way around.

I can't shake last night or the knowledge that every day Aria seeps deeper into my blood and every thought that I have.

I'm consumed by her. I can't deny it. She brings out a side of me that should have stayed dead.

"Are you listening?" Daniel asks me, tearing my eyes away from the drawing Aria made yesterday.

He looks as worn out as I feel. It's because of Addison. She's not okay being back here. She didn't realize what this family became after she left. Time changes everything, but she didn't know. She couldn't have. And this lockdown leaves us nowhere to hide.

"She needs more than this. She's not handling the transition well. She needs... she needs to not feel trapped." Daniel hunches over in his chair, both hands on the back of his head, his elbows on his knees. When he looks up at me, I feel like I truly am the monster Aria calls me for putting him through this. For putting both of them through this. With tears in his eyes, he tells me, "I'm losing her. I don't want this for her."

"You're protecting her," I remind him. She's the one they went after and tried to kidnap, to kill, to do whatever they wanted with. She may have been safe if he'd never chased her. If they hadn't realized he loved her. But you can't change the past.

"She doesn't care," he tells me as he swipes his eyes with the heel of his palm, hiding his pain with a look of anger and annoyance I know is just a ruse. "She thought at first I was overreacting. That it was all in my head and over the incident at her place." He shakes his head silently before looking me in the eyes. "She said I was being ridiculous. She had no idea. So, I had to tell her."

"You told her what?" I ask him, just now realizing he's told her more than she needs to know.

"That men are going to die, and those men want us dead first. I told her we're at war. She still wants out. She doesn't like this. And I don't like keeping her here against her will."

My voice feels tense and catches in my throat watching him in pain over this.

"She didn't agree to this. This wasn't what it was like when we were kids. She had no idea, and I brought her back blindly. I was selfish." His words are laced with regret. The last sentence comes out in a harsh whisper. "So fucking selfish." The pain radiates off of him. "I can't lose her again."

"You can't risk her safety either," I reply and I'm firmer with him than I usually am. We're at war, and Talvery and his men will attack us the moment they can. "If I were them," I tell Daniel, "I'd be waiting and any chance I could take to strike first, I'd take it."

"I know," he murmurs and hangs his head. "They know they're dead men; they have nothing to lose. And they'd kill her just because I love her."

"It'll all be over soon," I say to try to offer him comfort as he rests his elbows back on his knees and steeples his fingers, keeping them against his lips.

"I don't know if she'll still love me then," he whispers his pain.

"I know what you mean." The words slip out and I can't stop them. Daniel's eyes hold a question, but he takes a moment to ask it. Waiting and stretching the silence.

"Have you thought for a moment, that maybe keeping her locked up is putting her more at risk? There's only so much you can control for someone until it turns on you."

"What choice do I have?" I retort, and his gaze

moves to the floor again. "We're all prisoners of war," I remind him. "But it will be over soon."

"When it's done with... she'll stay? Aria will stay with you?" he questions me.

I search his face for the intention, why he would even consider her leaving.

"She won't hold it against you?" he asks me as if knowing what I needed to hear him say in order to answer.

"I don't know. She's mine. And she'll stay with me. Forgiveness will come."

He starts to say something, readjusting his footing but then he shakes his head.

"I came in to tell you something else, although I'm not sure you want to hear it," he tells me and straightens in his chair.

I gesture for him to go on. Although, I don't know why I'm in a rush. I've barely spoken to Aria this morning and I'm not sure I'm ready to, not after last night.

I expect him to tell me the same shit Jase has been saying, that Marcus is up to something. Marcus is going to strike. That we have three enemies now, not just one.

Without any proof other than the word of dead men. A single word. The enemies will fall in order: Talvery, Romano, and then Marcus. When we have more proof. I'm not in the habit of starting a war over a single word from the lips of a soon-to-be-dead addict.

"Nikolai is asking around for her," Daniel tells me and that catches me by surprise.

"Is that right?" I ask as my thumb taps against my lip. Resentment stirs inside of me. He brings out a side of jealousy in me that I've never felt before. *He had her first.*

Daniel nods with the hint of amusement at his lips. "Ever since Romano confirmed it."

"And what's he asking?"

"How he can get her back." He doesn't hide the thrill in his eyes from delivering this news to me.

"You're a prick for loving this as much as you do."

"It certainly adds an interesting dynamic, doesn't it?" he asks and a mix of curiosity, hate, and jealousy mingle in my blood.

"He has nothing to bargain with and even if he did, there's nothing I'd want in her place."

"He's already been told that and that it would be pointless to even ask you, but he *demanded* you be told."

"Did he?"

I can't blame Daniel for being so amused. "He seems to really care for her."

"Is this the first or second time I've told you I want him to die first?" I ask Daniel and he only snorts a laugh. Every night in the cell that Aria spoke his name, my hate for Nikolai grew. And she did it often. I'm fully aware of how *close* they were. Too fucking close for him to keep breathing when all of this is over.

"You really think she'll forgive you?" he asks with a cocked brow. I don't think he realized what his question would do to me.

She'll have to forgive me. There's no other way.

I DON'T like leaving Aria or being away from the estate right now, especially knowing that every moment I'm away is a moment that threatens to make her question what she should do. That's a dangerous thought to leave her with; all she should do is what I tell her, but I have to be present for this.

There are times when it's required to be seen. This particular instance is one of those times. With slicked-back hair and a sharp suit, Oliver looks younger than I remember him. Maybe it's the wide grin on his face that adds to his youthful appearance. Maybe it's the shot of what looks like whiskey that he clinks against Frank's beer and then throws back as he takes his seat. Neither of them sees me, but the security and Jared notice the moment I enter. They tense as I let the back doors close easily behind me, listening to Frank's hard slap on Oliver's back in congratulations.

Frank's all right I guess. He's a little older than me, only by a few years, but he's perpetually twenty-one. A punk kid with no goals in life other than making a buck on the streets and letting everyone know he's proud of it. I don't give a fuck what his motivation is, so long as he listens. I catch his light blue gaze and he slides back in his chair with a broad smile. "The boss is here," he utters but his jovial words are slurred.

"Your mom waiting up for you, Frank?" I ask him, hiding my grin as I walk toward the table they're sitting at in the right corner of the room.

Glancing over my shoulder, I take notice of who's

counting the money down the hall. All the drugs come in and out of the Red Room, Jase's nightclub. As does the money.

"Ma can wait up all she wants." He blows off my comment, not taking the hint that he should make his way out.

"I think there's some business," Jared points out and gestures between myself and Oliver, his head tilted as he tries to convey to Frank that he should get the fuck out of here.

The shot glass sounds heavy as it hits the table and Frank pushes out his chair. "All right, all right, the big guys gotta talk." He mutters without looking at me, "You don't got to tell me twice." As he's putting on his jacket, I lay a hand down on his shoulder and wait for him to look at me. I stand close to him, catching him off guard and creating a thick tension that's undeniable. Fear looms in the depths of his eyes as I tell him earnestly, not breaking eye contact, "Thanks for understanding."

"Can we get another?" Oliver asks, the happiness not at all dampened. He doesn't see how Frank stumbles backward; he doesn't notice the change in the air. Frank does, and all he says on his way out is, "Of course, boss."

Yeah, Frank's an all right guy.

As I pull out the chair across from Oliver, letting it drag across the floor, Frank leaves, entering back into the club, bringing in the pounding music. It's quick to fade as the door closes with a resounding click.

"Thank you, thank you," Oliver thanks Jared, who's

pouring out another shot of whiskey in front of Oliver and then filling the empty glass Frank just had.

"To finally snuffing out the fucking Talverys." Oliver's age finally shows as he raises the glass in the air and doesn't hide the hate on his face. He's new to the crew. Not at all like Frank, who started with me only five years ago. I picked up men as I took over street by street. Giving the men who ran them the option to come with me or die.

Oliver came to me though. Pissed that Talvery didn't want him, he offered up his services as muscle on the street. If it wasn't for Jared's word, I never would have hired him. Too old. Too cocky. More than that, he's too eager to make a name for himself.

With a nod of my head, the old man throws the drink back, clicking his tongue against the roof of his mouth as he sets down the glass and shakes off the burn of the shot.

"I heard everyone's ready to get it over with," I tell him, resting both of my arms on the table. A sly grin kicks up his lips. "Couldn't be more ready, boss."

My own grin shows itself. An asymmetric smirk as he calls me boss.

The dumb fuck should have remembered that earlier today.

"So, what happened," I ask him easily, motioning with my hand palm up for more, "give me all the details."

He's grinning from ear to ear as he tells me what I already heard, what *everyone* heard.

"There were four of them right across the street

from Dale's bar, on Sixth Street. I saw them walking in and knew they'd be there for a few."

In my periphery, I see Jared stiffen; he knows me well enough to realize that this isn't going to end well for the man he stuck his neck out for to get on the crew. I bet he's wondering what that means for him. If I was him, I'd be wondering too.

Oliver still hasn't caught on. He's nothing but proud as he tells me how he walked in and shot all four of them before they ever grabbed their guns.

"All on Talvery's turf? That takes balls." I compliment him although inside my heart is pounding, adrenaline raging inside of me and the tension building. I've been needing a release for all of this pent-up anger. Wiping the smirk off old Oliver's face might be exactly what I need. That, or falling back into bed with Aria.

Just the thought of having her makes me want to speed this shit up and get back to her.

I've already been gone long enough.

"No one's making a move, but they were right there," he says and emphasizes his words, shaking his hands in the air. No one's crossing lines, and no one's made a move, not even Nikolai. But this dumb fuck thought he could do it and get away with it.

"How many shots have you had so far?" I ask him, my foot tapping against the ground as my impatience grows with every thought of getting Aria under me tonight.

"This is my fifth since Jared brought me in." He

sways slightly in his chair as he tells me, but the smile only widens.

"Two for each of the four," I say loud enough for everyone to hear me and stand up. I have to walk around the table to pat him on the shoulder as I tell him, "Three more, all on me."

The smell of whiskey hits me hard as he reaches up to return the pat on my arm. His touch is firm with the first pat, but I don't stay in place, making the second one turn to a tap. My gaze is on Jared as Oliver says something behind me. A thanks and another cheers to killing the Talverys. I don't fucking care what the dead prick has to say.

Pausing in front of Jared, I keep my voice low as I tell him.

"It's on you to slit his throat when he's done those three shots."

On cue, Oliver calls out for another. The blood drains from Jared's face, but he nods and with a low voice he answers, "Of course."

There's not a hint of anything but remorse on Jared's face. He's tense, but he had to know it was coming. "No one does a damn thing until I say so." My shoulders stiffen, and the anger threatens to show itself, so I reach out, straightening Jared's tie and then add, "If there are any other dumb fucks who want to show off and not wait for my orders," I look Jared in the eye to tell him, "don't bother me and make me come in here. Kill the pricks where they stand."

CHAPTER 15

Aria

THE FRONT DOOR IS OPEN; it's never open.

The soft pads of my feet patter against the marble floor as I make my way to the entrance, following the bright light of day.

I can already smell the fresh air and the warmth before I step outside. The grass in the front yard is lush and although it's fall, the weather is lovely.

I haven't stepped on the porch at all. Not once since I've been here, and the thought seems too odd to be a reality, but it is. I was carried inside, and I've only ever looked through the etched glass of the windows but I don't try to do that often as it is. It just seems cruel to tease myself like that.

I glance behind me, down the foyer, and then peek

outside, but I don't see anyone. Not at first. Not until I take a step onto the smooth slate porch and then another.

I hear him first, Jase. With a phone to his ear, he walks around the side of the house and then back up. There's a hitch in my breath and a slam in my chest; I freeze, but only for a split second.

I'm walking outside.

I'm not trying to run away. Although I have to force my limbs to move, I do just that. Staring Jase in the eyes, I walk to the stairs. They're grand and massive, just as you'd expect for an estate like this. Not to mention beautiful. Everything about this place looks expensive and each detail intricate, from the trimmed bushes and groomed flower beds to the arched driveway paved with cobblestone, reflects an elegance from whoever lives here.

I nearly snort just thinking about Carter choosing all these details. Carter is anything but elegant.

I hold Jase's gaze as I slowly sit on the steps. A large column blocks me from his view and I can imagine he'll come running.

So sorry to interrupt his phone call. The captive is flee-ing; call the guards, call the guards!

A genuine laugh makes my shoulders shake at the sarcastic thoughts. As I lean against the column, enjoying the sun that dances across my skin and the fresh breeze, Jase comes running up the yard, just as I anticipated.

Rolling my eyes, I give him a face. A face that says, *are you fucking kidding me?*

"I'm on break from being the prisoner. I called in a temporary replacement," I mutter.

His lips twitch like he wants to smile, but he doesn't. He doesn't say anything, not to me and not for a few minutes. I can hear the sound of someone speaking from his phone although I can't make out the words. He doesn't seem to pay attention to them at all.

My heart beats a little harder and anxiety trickles slowly into my veins. My foot nervously taps on the stone steps, but I hold my ground. Even as I start to get emotional, knowing that I can't even step outside without someone losing their shit, I stay right the hell where I am and enjoy the fucking porch.

"I'll call you back," Jase finally speaks, although it's still not to me. My muscles get rigid and my teeth clench together. *If he thinks he's taking me inside...* I swallow thickly at the thought. What am I really going to do? I can at least kick him. One good hard kick, maybe in the shin. I nod my head faintly at the idea, keeping my eyes on a few leaves that have turned a beautiful shade of auburn as they sway in the gentle wind. If he puts a hand on me to force me back inside, I swear I'm going to kick his ass.

A soft grin tugs at my lips. It's nice to feel like a tough girl at least. And like I have a choice.

"You picked a good day," Jase says, and I lift my gaze to see him slipping the phone into his pocket before he climbs the first few steps to sit by me but on a stair lower than mine.

I'm quiet for a moment, gauging how he looks so

comfortable and acts like this is normal. Just like he did in the kitchen.

"It is nice." I nip at my lower lip before adding, "I used to have a balcony off of my bedroom. I liked sitting out there."

He glances back at me for a moment but ends it with a short, almost sad smile and then he leans back, bracing his forearms on the step behind him.

I guess my guard has decided to pretend to be my friend and just sit by me.

"Who designed this place?" I ask him, wanting a distraction and to think of anything but last night.

I woke up alone and that's exactly how I've felt all day. Miserable and alone.

I could sit peacefully in silence on my own, but Jase interrupted that. If he's going to babysit me, then he's going to have to talk to me. A punishment for a punishment. I smile at the snide remark in my head and think about raking up all the good lines I've had since I walked out here. I guess I'm in a bitchy mood. *Good luck to my adversaries.*

"We did," he answers with a smirk that doesn't hide his pride.

"No, you didn't." I don't even hesitate to call him out on his bullshit.

"Why would you think we didn't?" he asks me, a quizzical look on his face.

"You're telling me that you chose lilacs and peonies for the front yard?" I question him, challenging him to tell me that any of the Cross brothers wanted those plants.

Jase's expression turns guarded and he clears his throat as he looks toward the very bushes that give me my argument.

"Our mother wanted lilacs and peonies." His admission is spoken simply, flatly. "She asked for them for Mother's Day, but she died just before," he tells me, and his voice dims toward the end.

"I'm sorry," I say and keep my tone gentle. "I didn't mean-"

"It's fine," he says and waves me off. "I get what you mean, but yeah, we designed it. A few years back." A gust of wind blows by, sweeping some of my hair in front of my face and some behind my back, leaving a chill in its wake and reminding me that it is, in fact, fall.

"Well, it's beautiful," I tell him genuinely. I ignore the chill in the air and wrap my arms around myself. Goosebumps threaten, but I'm not ready to go back inside and the sun feels warm. I could lie in the sun all day, but it looks like I barely have an hour before the trees on the edge of the estate will hide it from me.

"You aren't planning on running, right?" Jase asks me and turns around to look at me with a stern look on his face. "I'd like to keep my balls, and I'm sure Carter would take them if I let you leave."

Laughter erupts from me just because of how serious he looks. His expression changes to one of humor and I find myself surprised by him yet again. Shaking my head, my hair tickling my shoulders I tell him, "Daniel told me it's useless with the guards." I shrug as if it's all a joke.

That's what my captivity is apparently, a fucking

joke. Yet, there's only a modest pang of despair from that thought.

Jase huffs and looks over to the right side of the yard. And the way he does it makes me think Daniel's lying. Like Jase is hiding something from me.

"There are guards?" I question him. "Aren't there?"

He looks me up and down for a moment like he's considering telling me something.

"Yeah," he nods and tells me, "we have a few posted along the fences."

I acknowledge what he said with a small nod, but don't respond. Instead, I think about taking a walk to clear my head, but I'm sure Jase would follow me like a lost puppy and I wouldn't be able to think anyway.

"We told them to just taze the pretty brunettes, though."

I give Jase's joke a small laugh and lean forward to run my hand down my legs before considering if he was being truthful. "You're joking?" I ask him, and he shrugs like an asshole with a shit-eating grin on his face.

"You're in a good mood today," I mutter sarcastically.

"Right back atcha."

Time passes easily for a moment, but much to my dismay the clouds come in and capture the sun before I'm ready for the warmth to leave me.

"You want a blanket?" Jase asks me, and I glance at him, watching as he stands up, stretching his back and wincing as he holds his ass. "You might want to bring a chair out too if you're staying longer," he tells me, and I can't help but smile.

"I may go in; I don't know," I tell him and that's when my dumb heart reminds me that I'll have to see Carter and that he's being weird and distant... and stupid and guarded and a fucking dick. My throat goes dry and I let out a distressed breath. I can't look at Jase when I do. I know he saw, though.

"You know he has it bad for you, right?" he asks me and that dryness in my throat travels higher, making me feel like I'll choke if I speak, so I don't.

"Don't hurt him," Jase tells me, and I whip my eyes to his, craning my neck since he's standing up now.

"Me?" I ask him incredulously. "First of all, I don't hurt people. Secondly, he won't let me close enough to even think of hurting him. Whatever we have is very one-sided and," I try to keep going, but my words crack, and I hate it. I hate that I'm emotional over this. I hate that I'm close to admitting how much I feel for him and that whatever he feels for me isn't even close to being the same. I get why Beauty fell in love with the Beast, but it doesn't change who Carter is. There's no magical rose or kiss that will turn him into a prince. All Carter will ever be is a beast.

That ragged breathing comes back, and I stand up, ready to make a cup of tea and go hide in the den, or maybe the new room, the white room, the pretty room with the replicas of what I used to be in it. Whatever the hell that gilded room is. My hideaway room.

"Hey, hey," Jase's voice is comforting, and he takes a

step closer to me, but doesn't touch me as he says, "He's had a hard time."

"Yeah, well, so have I." I bite out the words and surprisingly keep the bitterness in my voice to a minimum.

"He's had a decade of hard times, of people he loved dying, his only friend and brother leaving him, and then other fucked up shit. It was a never-ending cycle until he became the person he is now."

I glance up at Jase, but only for a second because I don't want to cry. He looks sympathetic at least, and genuine, but right now I need to know something will change. I don't need excuses; they're never good for anything.

"What are you doing out here?" Carter's sharp voice makes me jump and I nearly fall backward on the stairs but catch myself. My heart pounds and for the first time, I feel real fear since coming outside.

"Are you crying?" Carter asks me with disbelief and then turns to Jase with a look that could kill.

"She was just talking about you, actually," Jase answers Carter slowly, and the two stare at each other for a long, hard moment.

"I wanted some fresh air for a minute," I say to break up their *moment*, not holding back my anger as I continue. "I got lucky enough that my cage door was open." With those parting words, I step past both of them, brushing against Carter as I do and hating that I breathe in his scent, feel his warmth, and love them both.

I need a cup of tea, a good book if I can find one in

my new room, my hideaway room, and some time to ignore the world.

But Carter doesn't give me that. I make it two steps inside the door before he snatches my elbow. I rip my arm away and he looks at me like he doesn't understand. Like I'm the one who's acting out of the ordinary.

"What's wrong?" he asks me, concern lacing the demand to answer him.

"Are you fucking serious?" I don't contain my outrage even though I should have. Carter's eyes narrow and darken, but I don't let it stop me. My heart races and it hurts harder with each thump.

"You're being an asshole. An even bigger one than usual."

"Be gentle," I hear Jase say quietly as he shuts the front door, hiding the last bit of light from the day and leaving us with the sound of his trailing footsteps. Part of me wonders if he's talking to me or to Carter.

"I'm sorry," Carter says through clenched teeth, almost like those words weren't meant to come from him in this moment. He shifts his weight from his left to his right and looks down at me with a look that elicits both fear and that dark desire I can't deny.

A rumble of low irritation settles in his chest as he tells me, "Mind the way you speak to me."

"You should do the same," I bite back without thinking. But it's true. His eyes flash with anger, but he doesn't speak. His jaw is held firm and I bet if he were to clench his teeth any tighter, they'd break. "You treat me like a child," I tell him and then swallow thickly, feeling the knotted ball grow tighter in my throat. "You don't want me near you, you don't talk to me. And last night..." I can't finish because again I feel like I'm going to cry, and I swear I'm not going to. Not here.

He doesn't let me love him. But it's because I'm his whore. I already know that's the answer. It's why he didn't kiss me for as long as he did. I'm meant to be his whore and nothing more.

A moment passes where I'm just breathing. Staring into the eyes of a man who can make me feel so much, but right now it all hurts. I want him to hold me and let me hold him back. I want to slap him and tell him he's an asshole and that I hate him. I want him to tell me that he loves me, and he doesn't think of me like I think he does.

In a matter of seconds, I go through a fantasy where everything will be okay.

"Give me your hand," Carter commands me. I jut out my chin, hellbent on telling him to fuck off, but he has a pull over me. The depth of pain in the hollows of his dark eyes makes me bend to his will. Slowly, I bring my hand up for him to take it. Even if I am just his whore, obeying his command.

I watch as he presses my hand to his phone, flattening it and then turns his back on me, walking to a panel by the front door.

I can feel my eyebrows pinch together.

Carter already said he's sorry once. I doubt he'll say it again. At this point, I don't even know what I want him to say. His words aren't the problem, it's his actions.

"If you're going back outside, grab a coat." His words are stern but there's a trace of melancholy there. *Press your hand here*, he demonstrates. He gave me access. My heart flickers to life, and I hate that it does. It's the things like this that make me question what I am to him.

"I wasn't going back out tonight," I tell him weakly. Wanting more from him, but not knowing how much to push him. My eyes dart from his to the door. Carter's a hard man and maybe he's had a hard life, but I need more than what he gave me last night and today.

I don't know if I'm in a position to ask for it, to demand it, or if Carter is even capable of giving me more than this. And if he goes through with his plans, all of this is for naught.

"Well, whenever you do," Carter tells me but when my eyes reach his, he moves his attention back to his phone.

I glance down at what he's doing only to find him exit whatever it was and that's when I see today's date.

And that's when this little truce no longer matters.

Nothing matters.

CHAPTER 16

Carter

THE MORE I GIVE HER, the less I have her.

The moment I let her have access to outside, she stormed away from me. Not with the anger I expected given her outburst, but with a heartache that's inexplicable.

The color drained from her face and she ran from me. Literally ran away from me and straight to the white room. She ignored me when I called out to her and tried to muffle her cries.

Everything shattered in front of me. There was no sign, no warning.

It's my fault; she wasn't ready. I can't push her to move faster when the final deed has yet to be done.

That's the only thing I can think of that would make her run from me like she did.

Her door is locked, a feature I considered excluding, but I know I could knock it down if I needed to.

I haven't moved my eyes from the monitor on my phone but watching her cry hysterically on the floor was brutal. It was fucking torture.

It's been nearly an hour since she's stopped, but she hasn't moved from the floor. Sitting cross-legged and picking at her nails, she's just sitting there, rocking on and off, humming and crying. The only saving grace I have is that my necklace is still around her neck. She hasn't taken it off since I put it on her.

I told you to be gentle, Jase's text message interrupts the feed and I click over to it. He's the only reason I haven't lost my shit. Although I'm on the verge of ripping the door off the hinges of that room and demanding she tell me what set her off.

I fucking was. I quickly text him my reply and then add, *How much time has to pass before I can go in there?*

You can't. He answers immediately and even though a part of me knows he's right, a bigger part of me knows she needs me. She needs someone, and I want to be that someone.

What if we side with Talvery? Over Romano? I'm grasping at straws just to keep her.

It will be a sign of weakness. Jase's response is swift, and the next question is quick to come to my mind. I know no one will understand or respect why I'd allow Talvery to live. Not unless it's clear why. And undeniable.

What if I married her? I type the words, but I can't send them. The thought of her as mine truly, in every way, sends a thread of hope passing before my reach. So close, and so delicate, just like the necklace around her neck. And I think maybe she'd do it. She'd agree if I agreed to spare her family.

But being a wife to a monster only makes her vulnerable. The hope dies as quickly as the flame of a fire only meant to have an ember.

She's not feared, not respected. My enemies would kill her the first chance they got, just to hurt me. I know they would. Just as they tried to take Addison from Daniel.

Jase sends me another text. *She needs to tell you what happened.*

He's right. I need something to fix. Some way to control what went wrong.

If it's her family, you're fucked. Jase texts me again before I can text him back and I almost fling the phone at the wall when it shows on my screen. Instead, I flick to her monitor, but she's not there.

She's gone.

Just as I abruptly stand up, ready to hunt her down wherever she's gone off to, I hear her walking down the hall and slowly she comes into view.

Adrenaline spikes through me and I try to stay still. Because if I move, she might change her mind. She might go back to that fucking room, but I can't let her. I swear to God, I can't let her.

She enters the bedroom with bloodshot eyes, the hair

on the side of her face damp from her tears and her face reddened. Fuck, I've never felt pain like this. Even in the cell, she didn't cry like this. She's never cried like this.

It's as if she's mourning.

I can barely breathe, but I swallow the pain down as she steps into the room, refusing to look at me and then glancing at the bathroom.

"There's no bathroom in the other room. The hideaway room," she says, and her words are roughly spoken, but she doesn't cry.

"Come here." The command is soft, an attempt to comfort her. I know she likes being held and I can do that.

I can hold her better than anyone else can.

She walks numbly and when I wrap my arms around her, she doesn't react. She doesn't hold me or lean in. She doesn't stiffen either. She's just there. Her entire body feels frozen under my touch and I instantly pick her up, cradling her in my arms to put her into bed, to force her to rest and lie down with me. Everything will be all right in the morning.

But the second I take a step toward the bed, Aria jolts and slams her palms into my chest, kicking at the same time and deliberately falling out of my arms and crashing onto the floor.

"Fuck," I grunt out and reach down to help her up, but she scampers backward, crawling away from me before standing up again and facing me like a caged animal intent on running.

A thousand shards slice into every bit of me. Into

my numb skin, making their way inside my blood and up my throat.

"Aria, tell me what's wrong," I demand but she only shakes her head, pushing her hair away and then rubbing her hand against her tearstained cheek.

"You already know what's wrong," she says woefully, and I know I've failed her.

"You'll forgive me," I speak lowly, my hands clenching into fists.

Her eyes reach mine and they gloss over as she whimpers, "I know." She sniffles once and turns to go to the bathroom, but I can't let her.

"Tell me something," I say, raising my voice but she stops and then slowly turns. "Ask me anything," I add.

A moment passes where she only sways in the knee-length sleepshirt she's changed into. She almost says something twice, but in the end, she only shakes her head.

Finally, she asks me something I hate, but I know I deserve.

"Will I ever be allowed to leave?" Her question reflects her hopelessness.

"Yes." I want to tell her more, that I'll take her wherever she wants to go, but I'm afraid if I speak too much, she'll break down again. Every word has to be spoken carefully.

"When?" she asks.

"After the war is over," I tell her firmly. "There's no exception to that."

"And when will that happen?" Her words are small,

nearly insignificant, reflecting exactly how she must feel.

"Soon." I try to be short, not wanting to hurt her any more than she already is, but also not wanting to lie.

"I would like to at least say goodbye," she whimpers and her voice cracks.

"He knows where you are. If he wanted to say goodbye, he could."

"He knows I'm here?" The shock in her voice is unexpected and I feel like a prick. She's going to have the same reaction she did yesterday when she learned I had someone spying on her.

"Yes." I swallow thickly, but at least she's talking to me.

"And he hasn't come for me?" she asks with such sadness, but it only enrages me. Doesn't she know the man her father really is? He wouldn't risk his life for anyone. Not a damn soul. "How long?" She visibly swallows and hardens her voice as she asks, "How long has he known?"

"Since the dinner," I tell her and then count the days. "Four days."

Aria's face crumples and she covers her mouth with her hand, looking impossibly more dejected somehow.

"When you're at war, you eviscerate them first. I'm sure he has plans..." I want to lie to her, to tell her he has plans to get her after he's killed me. But I don't believe it. Talvery would bomb our estate, killing her with me, if he thought he could get away with it.

"Where does that leave me?" Aria asks in a weak whisper.

"What do you mean?"

"You're going to *eviscerate* the Talverys... where does that leave me?" she asks with surprising strength and tenacity.

"You belong to me." It's the only answer to that question. And the truth she already knows. She's already accepted it. I know she has.

"What would you do if I told you no? That I don't want you?" She steadies her breathing as best as she can and straightens her back. "That I don't want to be your whore anymore?"

"I would know you were lying. And you're not my *whore*." My heart pounds accompanied by a prickling along my skin.

I expect her to come back with some quip asking what she is to me then. But she doesn't. Instead, she tries to destroy what little goodness she's given me.

"What if things changed, and I didn't want you at all?" she asks me with each word clear and just as sharp as the knife it feels like.

"Why would you? Why would you *lie*?" I dare her to tell me it's the truth. That she doesn't want me anymore.

"You would have sent me back after the bath if I'd said 'no,' wouldn't you?" she asks me and I have to take a minute to realize what she's even referring to.

"Our first night? You didn't sleep with me because you wanted to stay out of the cell," I practically spit the words out of my mouth, brimming with outrage. "You didn't even know you weren't going back." My voice rises and I feel it scrape up my throat. "Your heels dug into my ass that night, spurring me on. You fucked me because you *wanted* me." I emphasize each word, taking a steady and dominating step closer to her with each one until I'm so close to her, I can feel the tension radiating from her. "You wanted to know what it would feel like to have my cock inside of you." Lowering my lips to hers I whisper, "Or am I wrong?"

She stares into my eyes and I stare into hers. The mix of greens and blues and golds are vibrant and alive amongst the shards of blotchy red and white.

"Did you want it or not?" I harden my question just as my gut twists with disgust and I start to question if she never wanted me at all. If I was so fucking obsessed with her that I was wrong all this time.

"Yes, I wanted you!" she screams at me although her last word crumbles before it leaves her lips. "And I shouldn't still want you." She doesn't hide the pain when she tells me, "I should hate you."

Relief, sweet relief, is short and minuscule, but there's so much relief in her admission.

"Why's that?" I ask her softly, wanting her to keep going. To work through this because, in weeks, this fight will be meaningless. She'll forgive me. She already knows she will.

"Because you're going to kill my family and everyone I love. That's why." The fight leaves her with the last sentence.

"Yes." I keep my voice strong, although I don't know how. "I am."

"Please don't," she whispers her plea and I wish I'd already done it. I wish I'd already shot the bastard, so she would stop this.

"Is your father a good man?" I ask her, knowing this is going to hurt her, but she's already so low, there's not much lower a little more truth can take her. "Do you think the men who protect him deserve to live long enough so they can try to kill me?"

"They won't," she tries to tell me, shaking her head vigorously and reaching out to take my hand with both of hers but I rip it away. I won't let her beg for his life.

"They've already tried," I say, and my nostrils flare as I tell her. "Right after his drug addicts killed my father. They murdered him for forty dollars and a bag of pills." I remember how my father looked on the metal table in the morgue. How his knuckles were bruised from fighting back.

"And your father was pissed that I dared step onto his turf to kill them. To get revenge. He protected them!" I scream at her and wish I hadn't. Tears flood from her again and she gasps for air. "Your father sent four men to our house. Our rundown, piece of shit house. The house my mother died in. The house you love so much." I can't help but sneer at the thought. "We weren't there. Thank fuck we weren't there."

She's barely breathing through her hands that are covering her face as if they can shield her from the hard truth as I tell her, "He had them burn it down with incendiaries. I should have killed him then, but I couldn't get to him. I sure as fuck can get to him now."

"I'm so sorry," she whimpers, and tries to calm

herself down. And I almost reach for her, to hold her, because I want to. Right now I need to hold her too. But then she speaks.

"Things have changed," she offers weakly, wiping the tears from her eyes although they don't stop flowing.

"How can you still defend him? After all this?" The pain won't fucking stop. I'm bleeding out the pain.

"The odds of me allowing your father to live are slim to none. Even if I want you to be happy, you know why he has to die. I bet you even think he deserves it," I tell her. "A small part of you has to think he deserves it."

"You said you'll kill them all, but all of them don't deserve it," she continues to plead with me, not offering me any comfort as I try not to break down remembering the soot and ash that stood in place of the home I'd grown up in. "It's not just my father who will die. Nikolai was my only friend. And my family will stand with my father. You can't kill everyone I've ever loved."

"If they stand against me, they deserve to die."

"Not all of them-"

"Like who? *Nikolai*," I sneer his name with disdain and she flinches.

"Please?" she begs me, but the loss is already clear in her eyes.

I turn my back on her, feeling lonelier than I've felt since she came into this house as I say, "You can make new friends."

CHAPTER 17

Aria

IT'S MY BIRTHDAY, but it wasn't until I saw Carter's phone that I knew what the date was.

No one here knows it's my birthday; why would they? They also don't know that yesterday was the anniversary of my mother's death. The day before my birthday.

And for the first time, I didn't go to her grave.

I start to cry again, and I don't know if I'm crying for my mother, for my family, or for Carter and the boy he used to be. I could cry forever, and it wouldn't be enough for the tragedy our families combined have suffered.

My back leans against the wall of the bathroom. To my left, the door is shut and in front of me, the shower is running to drown out the sounds of me crying. I wanted a shower to wash it all away. A hot, scalding shower.

Instead, I'm crouched on the floor by the door. I can barely stand, I'm so lightheaded and exhausted. I don't trust myself in the shower. I don't trust myself or anyone else anymore.

I know my father is a horrible man. A godawful man condemned to hell. I didn't know what he did to Carter. I had no idea. "I didn't know," I whisper to no one. I was so blind for so long and I wish I could go back. I hate all of this. I hate all the pain. I hate that there's no way to go backward.

I can already accept my father's death, as cruel as it sounds. For what he's done, there's no mercy in his death. More than that, he lived when my mother died. And he knows I'm here, yet he's done nothing. Nothing was ever done for my mother's murder. I'm sure my father would do nothing to honor my death.

Flames along the side of the house I've drawn flash before my eyes. I can't forgive him. I can't forgive my father, and I don't even want to know when he's gone. I don't want to give him the honor of mourning him.

But it's not just him.

It's Nikolai too. Why hasn't he come for me? Please, he can't be the same man my father is. A staggering breath leaves me. I know he's not, and I can't accept it.

I won't.

I've never felt so torn—no, so ripped apart.

But I'm sick of crying. I'm sick of dealing with death, time and time again. I'm my father's daughter. I live in a world where attachments are limited and mourning only fuels hatred. I've stayed hidden and quiet, attempting to go unnoticed for years and stay out of the way, and therefore, out of the sights of men who would see me as a bargaining chip. Yet, here I am, in the hands of a man hellbent on murder and vengeance.

But as I thought about how every anniversary of my mother's death, Nikolai brought me to her grave, I started to despair. How every birthday, I woke up finding a text from him and a note that he would take me wherever I wanted to go.

And how that didn't happen this time.

And how it never will again, and there was no way I could stop it.

There's no way I can save him.

I mourned the death of a man who still breathes. Not being able to hear him today or talk to him and let him know how I miss him and wish I could do something to stop it all, is a death in and of itself. And in its place is what I've been taught to hold my entire life. Hate.

It's as if Carter's already killed him; he's taken my only companion in this world away from me. And the anger in that realization grows by the second. Hardening my heart.

Maybe next year, when I visit my mother's grave, Nikolai's will be near.

The thought and visions of an old gravestone next to a newly carved one bring a new flood of tears.

That's all I can do. To mourn them.

To mourn us all. And to cling to my hate for a man I'm growing to love.

A soft click causes my eyes to lift to the doorknob and I watch it slowly turn. Haphazardly wiping my eyes, I slowly rise to my feet, leaning against the wall as Carter opens the door. Steam that fills the room drifts to the open space and the hot air makes my heated face feel that much hotter.

Carter stops after one step in the room, staring at the empty shower for a moment before turning to me when I let out a heavy and broken breath. The look in his eyes showed true fear until it settled on me.

I saw fear in the eyes of a man who does nothing but revel in it.

Still, I feel like nothing beneath him as he stares down at me. "I thought you were in the shower." His eyes roam my face, searching for something.

I try to swallow, but I can't. Instead, I shake my head softly and pray for him to leave. I should have stayed in the hideaway room.

"I don't like to see you like this." Carter's statement sounds genuine, but all I can give him in return is a sick and sarcastic huff of a laugh. It croaks from me and I can barely breathe in after. Reaching for the tissues by the sink, I turn my back to him. My shoulders are still shuddering with the mess of sorrow that weighs down on me.

His large hand settles down on my shoulder, carefully, gently, and he tries to pull me close to him. To hold me like he's done before. With half a step forward, he attempts to hug me from behind, he even closes his eyes and lowers his lips to kiss my bare shoulder.

But I'm quick to turn, push him away and step out of his embrace. He can't hold me and think it makes it all go away. Not anymore.

The tissue is balled in my fist as I push him again, shoving him away.

He doesn't let me comfort him, so I won't let him do the same to me. To use my pain against me. So, he can do as he pleases, regardless of the consequences they hold for me.

"No, you don't get to touch me." My words come out sharply with a fierceness I didn't know I still had in me. Rage heats in his dark eyes as his expression hardens and he stills where he is, his jaw tense and his shoulders rigid.

"Tell me now that you don't want to throw me back in my cell." Again, emotion cracks my words. I stare back at him, waiting for a response. It's difficult not to see the sorrow and fear in his gaze that he's showed me before.

"The only place I want to throw you is on my bed to remind you of what I can give you." He speaks quietly, in a deep tenor that sounds raw to my ears. "You still belong to me," he reminds me.

My lips twitch up into a sad smile. Sad for him that he thinks he could possibly ever have me the way he wishes. It will never happen.

A flicker of anger, the cluck of his tongue, one step toward me, and Carter morphs back into the man I recognize from weeks ago. Cold and calculated.

But you can't go back. He, of all people, should know better.

"Kneel," he commands but I can hear the desperation in his voice. He may want to pretend but he knows can't control me when I'm like this. I can barely control myself.

"Send me back to the cell." My demand comes out strong and with defiance, no one could deny.

I'll be better in the cell. Better there than the hideaway where I'm simply avoiding him. The cell leaves me no options. I need it. I need to get away from the man standing in front of me.

If Carter touches me, I'll cave. I know I will. I'll forget the pain and the anger. I'll forget to mourn. There will be nothing of me left but what he wants there to be.

I'm weak for him. "I need to be away from you," I whisper with harsh anger on my tongue.

"No." His denial of my request should only strengthen my resolve to disobey. But my limbs feel weak, and I so desperately need to be held. I want him to be the man to do it.

"Do I need to try to run?" I ask him in an obstinate breath, not daring to look him in the eyes.

"As if you could get away from me." His answer comes out softer than it should. And with more comfort than I can resist.

"Fuck you," I spit out at him in a last-ditch effort.

"You really want to go back to your cell, don't you? I could always keep the door open if you prefer. So you can pretend I'm the monster you want me to be."

I could always keep the door open. The words force tears to my eyes. He would take it away. Take away the pretense that I have absolutely no choice. Instantly, I hate him for doing this to me.

"I hate you," I spit at him, every bit of anger and sadness mixing into a deadly concoction.

Carter's eyes blaze with heat in the mix of all of this as he steps closer to me. With each step forward he takes, I take one in reverse until the back of my knees hit the edge of the tub.

"Admit it," he whispers so closely to me I can feel how hot he is. The hot water sprays down behind me, filling the room with white noise and heat. I can't take my eyes from Carter's as he leans in closer. His shoulders cage me in and his angular jaw holds nothing but dominance as he tells me, "Admit that you understand, and you know this has to happen. Admit it," he asserts.

"There's always a choice." I barely get the words out as he touches me. As he lays a finger, a single finger on my collarbone and lets it travel lower. His touch is fire to my skin. And I'll be damned if I don't want more of it. When my eyes reach his again, my heart twists with unbearable pain. The sadness conveyed in his expression reflects his low tone as he utters, "It's comforting to think we have choices."

When his eyes lift from my throat, where his finger travels up and down in a soothing stroke, the pain in his expression vanishes and once again the hardened man commands me, "Admit it. And admit you're mine."

Slap! I can't explain why I did it, even as my hand stings with severe pain, my lungs refuse to move, and fear overwhelms my body. A bright red handprint marks Carter's face and slowly he tilts his head back up to face me.

I slapped him. I struck Carter Cross.

One breath and he grabs both my wrists and shoves them above my head.

"Carter." The way I say his name is like a plea although I don't know what I'm begging for. I'm in over my head, feeling lightheaded and full of nothing but fear. Fear of him, of what's to come. Of everything.

"Aria," Carter's voice is strangled and reflects exactly how I feel. I open my eyes to beg him for forgiveness, to apologize, but his eyes close and he crashes his lips to mine.

Pressing them deeply to mine with a savagery I need to feel, nipping my bottom lip, devouring me until my own lips part and my tongue seeks his.

Fuck. I need this. I need him.

His fingers tighten around my wrists and he stretches them higher as his other hand roams down my body.

I don't know at what point the mourning and defiance changed to this. To the absolute need to be fucked by him, worshipped by his body. The feel of his powerful hold and brutal touch that turns soft the instant I need it to be, is addictive.

It's worse than any drug.

His left hand nearly releases my wrists, but the second I try to move, he tightens them again. "Carter," I say, and his name is a strangled moan as I squirm against the hard wall while his right hand finds my panties and shreds the lace. The thin fabric falls down my leg, tickling me in its wake and during all this, every nerve ending in my body is on edge.

"Aria," Carter moans my name, his scruff scratching my shoulder as he breathes against my neck. I'm so hot. Everything is hot and ready to be lit aflame.

His thick fingers drag along my pussy, the moisture there aiding in how easily they travel up to my clit then back down to my entrance. Pausing each time to tease me and bring me closer to the edge.

"Tell me you don't want me, that you're really done with me and I'll stop," Carter whispers and then drops his head to the crook of my neck. All I can hear is the mix of our heavy breathing and the white noise of the shower behind us.

My eyes open as I shudder and try to breathe, to make sense of any of this, and that's when I see us in the mirror. A sad, ragged girl with red eyes and nothing but pain reflected in them. Pinned to the wall by a man built to consume and bred by this world to hate.

And my heart breaks.

It breaks for both of us.

I don't want to cry anymore. "Please," is the only whimper I can manage, and I don't know what I'm pleading for.

Maybe just to take the pain away, if only for a little while.

Carter's strong chest presses hard against mine, trapping me and overwhelming me as he shoves his fingers deep inside of me while ravaging every inch of exposed skin with his lips.

I heave in a breath; my neck bows and my body rocks with the immediate pressure building deep in my belly. It rocks through me like waves. So close and threatening.

My nipples harden and my toes curl, my hips threaten to buck, to move away knowing the heavy hit is coming. But with Carter, there's nowhere to run. And the pleasure is an onslaught, an unforgiving bliss I'm submerged in.

My body is paralyzed by the blinding pleasure, and it's only then that Carter releases me. He doesn't let me sag against the wall, he immediately grabs my body, hugging me to him until he can lower me to the floor and shove his pants down.

He fucks me like it's the only thing he's ever wanted.

He takes his time, although each thrust is punishing.

I claw at his back and he bites my shoulder.

I scream out his name and he screams out mine.

Neither of us breathing, save the air from each other's lungs.

The heat, the passion, the need... it's all undeniable. I can admit that. Of everything Carter wants me to admit, I can admit that he has a part of me I didn't know existed and a part of me no one else will ever have.

"How can I hate you and love you at the same time?" I ask him in staggered words as I struggle to breathe. My eyes open wide, realizing what I said, but

Carter either doesn't hear or doesn't care as he climbs off of me, his cum leaking from me as I lie on the cold floor, panting.

A part of me cracks as he stands and runs his hand over his face and then down the back of his head. Standing with his back to me, a part of me shatters. I'm such a fool. A foolish girl at the whim of a monster. Lost in my pain until he can overpower it with pleasure.

HE CARRIED me to his bed. Wordlessly.

He wiped between my legs with a warm, damp cloth and then carried me to his bed. I can't look at him; I can't do anything but lie here. And every tick of the clock makes me wonder if I should climb out and go sleep on the floor of the hideaway.

My heart hurts too much.

At least he's not touching me. Every time the bed groans and the covers shift over my naked body I tense, thinking he's going to hold me, but he doesn't.

I replay the last twenty-four hours over and over again.

"Why did you look scared when I wasn't in the shower?" I finally ask him, breaking the silence and the pretense that I could even try to sleep. "I don't understand." I give him the reasoning for the question as it came seemingly from nowhere. They're the only words that have been spoken between us since the slap, apart from the confession that went unheard.

"Jase had a lover once," Carter answers me, softly spoken, but rough and deep. I can hear him breathe heavily, feel it even with the dip of the bed and then he adds, "She killed herself in the shower."

My lips part, although I stay lying on my side, my back to him. More pain. More tragedy. I wonder what Jase did to her that made her kill herself. I didn't think he was capable of such a thing. The question is on my tongue, but I don't ask it.

Carter had fear in his eyes when I wasn't standing in the shower because for a moment, for one brief moment, he thought I was lying dead in the tub.

CHAPTER 18

Carter

I WONDER if she really loves me.

I'll never forget the way she said it. It gutted me. She may grow to love me, but she'll always hate me.

I can't blame her for that, but I want to hear the words apart from the hatred. So, I can pretend it comes without a caveat.

I want her to say it again, and this time to mean it. Those words shouldn't have fallen so recklessly as I pushed her to the edge of pleasure. They're addictive and they did something to me I can't describe.

She's drawing so slowly today. Lying in front of the fire in the den, she's only been working on one picture. One single piece of art for the last three hours. I'm still not sure what it is, all I can make out is a field of flowers, but there's something beyond the black smudges of petals.

I don't have time to question her about it though. Other questions are too precious to be wasted by another moment of silence.

"What do you want more than anything in the world?" The fire crackles once my deep voice has broken the void of silence between us. The tension is still there, but it can't exist forever. I won't let it.

Aria's hazel eyes lift, and she peeks at me through her dark lashes, not bothering to move from lying on her elbows. She glances back at the drawing and visibly swallows before shrugging slightly and looking back up at me as if she doesn't have to answer.

At this point, she doesn't. I don't care what she does or how she treats me with the door closed, so long as she doesn't run or hurt herself.

"I want my family to be untouchable," I confess to her.

"That's quite an ambition," she answers, crossing her ankles and still staring at the drawing pad in front of her. She's still cold.

"Isn't that what you want, too?" I ask her. "That would seem to be especially desirable given the current environment." I can't keep the smug tone from my voice to cover up the pain from her reaction. If she would talk to me, she'd see. She has to see that there's only one way for this to end. And once it's over, it will all be better. I'll make it better for her.

"I want everyone to fuck off and leave me alone," she answers with a bite that tips the corner of my lips up into a half smile. I love the fight in her. She'll live, she'll survive. A girl like her knows how to survive if nothing else.

"Anger is something I didn't expect. And someone like you shouldn't be left alone," I tell her.

"I don't want to cry today. So, I'll settle for anger." Her answer comes with muted irritation. She throws down the stick of charcoal onto the paper and then meets my gaze to ask, "Why shouldn't I be alone?"

"It's one thing to say you want to be alone. It's another to truly be it. You pretend like you don't exist in the same world as I do. Locking yourself away and acting like that's what you want. But you belong here. You were born to this life. You need to accept that. And loneliness in this world leaves you vulnerable and that's a life neither of us can afford."

"I was alone in the cell," she says solemnly. I don't think she slept at all last night; I know I didn't. "I survived."

A melancholy huff leaves me. "You weren't alone. The first night you slept, I'd drugged your dinner to make sure you would. So, I could tend to your wounds and the cuts on your wrists."

"You did?" Her eyes are filled with shock. "Why?"

"You were mine to take care of." My shoulders stiffen, as does my gaze and she drops hers, falling back to the smudges of charcoal. "I knew you would live. And you would break quickly. Everything needed to happen quickly."

"Why?" she asks me, and I don't know how she can't know at this point.

"I'd intended to show how willing you were to be mine to everyone who was watching. So, there would be no question where you stood in the war."

Her eyes close and she chews the inside of her cheek at my admission, trying to keep her emotions in check. I know the truth of the situation is raw for her. An open wound. But she needs to see it all. She has to accept everything for what it is.

"Instead, there's no question where I stand when it comes to you. I never liked Stephan. Once a traitor, always a traitor. But giving his death to you, allowing you to have vengeance? It spoke more words than I realized it would."

Her face scrunches with the painful memory and then she hangs her head, avoiding my gaze and rubbing her cheek against her shoulder. She pushes the hair out of her face and when she speaks, she doesn't look up.

"But you're still going to..." She doesn't bother finishing her question. I know she already knows. She'll come to accept it.

"Your father doesn't deserve what he has. He's not half the man Romano is. And Romano is a pathetic excuse for his title. They'll both die. Along with everyone who fights for them."

"Please. Not everyone. I'll do anything." Her words are spoken with conviction and she lifts her hazels up to meet my dark gaze. "You want me to kneel at your feet? I'll kneel."

She still doesn't get it. And my heart aches for hers.

"What if I wanted you to stand at my side?" I ask her, my heart racing in my chest. It's a risk to give her more. Every time I do, she fails to cope with it. But I need her to know what I really want from her. What I desire more than anything.

"You would tower over me," she answers.

"That's not how it works, songbird. And it's not what I want. You've only ever had broken wings, but I can show you what true freedom is."

"You're still going to kill my family?" she asks me as if that answer is the end all, be all.

"I'm going to do a number of things you're going to disapprove of. You need to accept that." My answer is hard, leaving no room for any intolerance. "I'm not a good man."

"Is this what it would be like to stand by your side? To have no control and to simply accept what you do?" I'm surprised by her answer but eager to discuss terms.

"On some matters, you'll never have control, and you'll have to accept what I choose. Whether or not you want to know about them is your decision." I know part of her despair is because she knows everything, yet she's a casualty with little recourse.

"I'm sorry you know as much as you do," I tell her and then almost take it back, thinking she'll take it offensively and that's not what I intended.

She doesn't though. Instead, she cracks, showing me the side of her I love. The raw vulnerability.

"I don't want this life," she whispers, slowly pushing the art away so she can rest her head against the rug. The light from the fire licks along her skin.

"We don't get to choose," I remind her. I've told

myself so many times that I wish things were different, but you live the life you're given.

"You're wrong," she tells me as if she has another option.

"Do you love what I do to you? How I fuck that pretty little cunt and force you to scream out my name?" I'm crude and harsh with my question.

She doesn't answer me, but she doesn't have to.

"Then no, you don't have a choice. I had a choice once. I chose wrong."

"You'll get tired of me," she whispers, her eyes seemingly vacant but the depths of them harboring pain. "One day I won't be a shiny new toy. One day, you'll want someone to fight you and I'll have none left in me." Tears pool in her eyes. "One day, the idea of shoving your dick inside of me won't interest you in the least."

She has no idea how wrong she is. I'm only growing more obsessed with her. Breaking every rule to satisfy her.

Risking everything to heal the broken pieces of her she refuses to acknowledge.

I'll never let her go because she isn't a toy. She isn't a challenge. She isn't the fuckdoll she thinks she is and secretly loves being.

"Will you let me go then?"

"Never."

She turns to face the fire and I whisper to her, "You're so wrong, Aria. If you weren't so set on hating me, you'd see."

"You give me every reason to hate you," she tells me.

In the reflection from the mirror above the mantel, I see the fire dancing in her eyes.

She'll never know how much her words hurt me. Or maybe she does, and that's what she was after.

"Why are you doing this to me? Why me?" she asks me in a single breath and I offer her a singular truth in return.

"Your father set a series of events in motion," I reply, remembering the night his men took me from the street.

I remember how the pills spilled into the gutter even as they slammed their fists against my jaw and I fell to the cold cement. With her, I only see what lies ahead. But she's caught in the past. And that's what will destroy us.

"So, it's my father's fault?" she asks me with a sadness in her eyes, as if I've robbed her of some fantasy.

"No, it's mine." My confession confuses her for a moment, but before she can say anything else, I continue.

"I thought I loved you," I tell her with a bitter hardness that forces the words to sound violent on my tongue. Her eyes widen as she turns back and stares at me. Her stance changes to one of prey, realizing it's stumbled into its worst enemy. The shock in her eyes fuels me to push her farther. For her to realize the man I truly am.

"For a long time after I left your home, when they kicked me back out onto the street after brutalizing me, I thought I loved whoever belonged to the sweet voice that stopped them from killing me." Aria's expression changes to one of fear and knowing.

I tell her to break whatever thoughts she has of love. And whatever thoughts I have of it. Weakness crushes down on me as I tell her what I used to think. What I expected this to be when I stabbed the knife into her picture and told Romano to bring her to me.

"I knew I hated your father, and eventually I hated everything. I hated you for letting me live." Aria is silent, waiting with bated breath to see what else I'll say.

"I'm condemned to hell. Of everyone on this Earth, God knows I deserve to burn. And it's because I was allowed to live. It's because of you."

"It has nothing to do with me. My father--"

"It has *everything* to do with you," I tell her, feeling the rage from the memory take over. "You're the one who banged on the door and pleaded with your father. I was so foolish. For a long time, I thought when you were crying out, 'I need you,' that in some fucked up way, you were calling out for me."

As I take another step closer to her, the wildness returns to Aria's eyes, the fear I know and love swirls within them. Her cunt is still feeling the pleasure I give her, while her heart beats with the knowing fear of me.

"I didn't--" she starts to protest, and I stop her.

"You're the bird in the forest who lured the child out of safety until he fell into a black hole he could never get out of. And still, the bird sings so beautifully, taunting the child as he becomes a man of hardness and hate, stuck in a hell he didn't know was coming.

Do you know what that man dreams of more than anything?" I ask her, remembering the moment my gratitude changed to hate for the very girl who sits in front of me.

She barely shakes her head, not taking her gaze from me.

"First to get out, for the longest time, just a way to get out. But when he realizes he can't, that there's no changing who he is and where he's damned to, he searches for the songbird. Eager to capture it. Just to silence the song forever. That's why I wanted you."

I lean forward, pinning her with my gaze as I tell her, "Aria, that was before I held you. No matter how much you choose to hate me, I swear I'll never let you go. You mean so much more to me than I would dare to admit to anyone."

CHAPTER 19

Aria

BANGED ON THE DOOR.

The stove ticks with the flame licking up from the burner and I turn it to medium before setting the pot of water on it.

I can't get over Carter's confession.

I would never go to the half of the estate where my father does his business. My mother died on the second floor in that half of the house and I swear I can still feel her there.

Whatever he thinks happened, didn't.

I never interrupted my father's work or even attempted to be anywhere near his business. I never banged on the door. I never called out that I needed anyone for anything.

I wouldn't dare.

Carter chose wrong. The woman who called out to him and saved him... she wasn't me.

I'm not his songbird luring him into the forest. I'm not the girl he thought he loved yet grew to hate.

It was never supposed to be me.

The hollow emptiness I've felt since he left me there in the den all alone, is unexplainable. I should be happy; I should tell him how wrong he was to take me. I should confess that voice he heard didn't belong to me. Instead, I swallow the dark secret down and let it choke me as I watch the pot of water boil.

"What are you making?" Daniel asks me and disrupts my thoughts. "Damn, you look like hell," he says, scratching the back of his head. In bare feet, faded jeans, and a plain white t-shirt, he looks relaxed, but he can't hide the exhaustion in his expression.

"Ditto," I tell him and spoon the potatoes into the pot. I've already cut everything else I need to make potato salad. Now I just wait. My mother used to make the best potato salad. I swear it's better the day after though, once it sits in the fridge for a full night.

I'm not hungry at all. I'm simply going through the motions, pretending the truth of my situation doesn't destroy every fiber inside of me.

Daniel opens the fridge as I spoon in the last few chunks. With the door open and his face hidden from me as he reaches for something, he asks me, "Want to talk about it?"

A genuine, yet sad smile tugs at my lips.

"You want to talk about *your* problems?" I ask him back.

"I asked you first," he says with a hint of humor, shutting the door and revealing a jug of orange juice.

"You sound like your brother," I tell him absently.

"Well shit," he tells me, pulling out a glass. It clinks on the counter as he smiles at me. "Don't go offending me left and right there, Aria," he jokes, and I let the small laugh bubble up although it sounds subdued and futile.

I stir the hard potatoes even though I know I don't need to. But I completely forgot the timer, and the realization makes me lean forward to start it.

With the beep of it being set, and the numbers counting down, I take a step back and lean against the counter.

"What'd he do this time?" Daniel asks me, mirroring my position as he leans on the other side.

"Nothing new," I tell him and the honesty in those words is what hurts the most.

The soft smile that lingered on his lips vanishes at my reply, and so I focus on the numbers, watching them as if I could speed them up if only I stare hard enough.

"Why won't he let me leave?" I ask him in a whisper.

Because he thinks you're someone else. Someone who saved him.

My throat dries, and my words crack as I tell him, "This isn't right."

It's silent for a long while, with only the sound being the water beginning to boil again.

"Because he cares for you," Daniel finally says, and I look him in the eyes, letting him see the real effect Carter Cross has on me.

"What a way to show it. Killing my family is just the cherry on top." My sarcastic response makes Daniel's expression harden.

"I have opinions of your father as well," he tells me softly, in a tone I haven't heard from him yet. My heart slams once and I'm forced to look him in the eyes. "I'll keep them to myself though," he tells me and then opens the fridge to put the orange juice back.

No doubt so he can leave me. So he doesn't have to tolerate my self-pity.

"And what about everyone else? Everyone I've ever known and loved?" I can barely breathe as I push him for justification.

"If you knew the truth," he tells me, facing me after shutting the fridge doors, "you wouldn't blame him." There's so much sincerity from him, I almost question my resolve.

"It's not just my father. So, I can, and I will blame him," I respond despondently, although I'm undecided on whether or not I believe my own words. When I look up at Daniel, my heart races chaotically and my body freezes.

Addison walks into the kitchen slowly, glancing from Daniel to me before offering me a small smile.

I can't breathe, and I don't know what to do. Anxiety pricks at my skin as she takes me in. My hair is still damp from the shower and I'm wearing a sleep shirt. I know my eyes show the lack of sleep and I look like a fucking mess.

More than that, I know Addison doesn't know who I am. She's normal. She's not forced to stay here like I am. Not the same way, at least.

Daniel plays it off far better than I do, wrapping his arm around Addison and giving her a soft kiss that forces her eyes back to him.

Shifting my weight, I glance at the timer and consider just leaving. I don't know what I'd say to her if I could even look her in the eyes right now.

Hi Addison, I know all about you and I know you don't know anything about me. I'm Carter's whore and he's going to kill my entire family soon, so I'm not allowed to leave. Nice to meet you.

Although that's not quite true. He admitted I mean more to him. *But it's because he thinks I'm someone else.* I've never felt more shame than I do right now. Every time I remember his words, I want to cry. Because he never wanted me and the moment he finds out the truth, he'll throw me away.

"Addison," Daniel's voice breaks up my spiteful thoughts as he says, "This is Aria. She's with Carter."

She's with Carter.

His words echo in my head as Addison smiles sweetly, pushing a lock of hair behind her ear and giving me a small, but friendly wave while staying where she is. "It's nice to meet you," she says kindly although she glances back at Daniel, no doubt wondering what's wrong with me.

"Hi," I offer up a single word and it croaks. I'm not

with Carter; I'm against him. Except of course when I'm writhing underneath him.

"She's having a hard day," he tells her softly. My heart thumps in the way that hurts. The way that makes it feel like it's a tight ball that needs air and without it, it only gets tighter.

"Sorry." I swallow and tell her, "I'm not usually this weird." I roll my eyes and force a huff of a laugh up to ease the tension.

"You're not weird," she says and shakes her head at my words. "Just looks like you're having a hard day. That's totally reasonable," she adds with her hands waving out in front of her. "No judgment here."

I get the feeling that Addison is lonely from her tone, from her awkwardness. Or maybe I'm just projecting what I feel myself.

"Let's get back," Daniel says and the tightness in my throat grows. At least I got to meet her, and he said I'm with Carter. It's respectable. Well... to some. I'm sure to her it is.

"Sure," she tells him softly, with an answer spoken so low it's just for him, but then she raises her voice and speaks to me.

"Do you want to come with me to the gym tomorrow?"

I blink at her question. I'm surprised by it and not sure what to say.

"I just took a shower, so..." she starts to say and then rocks on her heels, wrapping her long hair around her wrist nervously.

I don't know if I'm even allowed to talk to her

alone. Anger rises inside of me. I don't need permission. And one day, she'll know what I am and why I'm here. I can't hide it forever. Then what will she think of me?

"I don't know," I offer her. My gaze flickers to Daniel, but he stands easily beside Addison as if nothing's wrong. Like none of this is abnormal. The way the Cross boys do.

"Come on, we can drink wine while we do the back thing. It feels good," she says playfully. "I don't even like working out," she says and then looks at Daniel as if looking for permission, but not waiting for any. "But being locked up here is killing me and it's at least something different to do."

I watch the happiness drain from her and the smile only staying where it is because she's forcing it. "If you want company, I could really use some girl time," she says softly and then rolls her eyes as the emotion plays on her face. "Sorry," she huffs, shaking her head and leaning into Daniel as he holds her close. "I'm having a bad day too."

"I can work out," I tell her immediately, saying what she wants to hear just to take away her pain. I bite my lip as my heart sputters, wondering if Carter will stop me from going.

"I'm not a runner though," I warn her, trying to lighten the mood and force a small smile to my lips.

A genuine happiness lights up her face and she nods enthusiastically. "Oh, yeah, for sure." She laughs a little and breathes out easily, "If you ever see me running, you should start running too because there's someone behind me trying to get me," she jokes and doesn't see how Daniel responds. How his lips turn down and then press into a thin line. She's oblivious to it, but when she glances at him, he's quick to hide it. To offer her a peck of a kiss and then tell me although he's still looking at her, "I'm surprised she's using the gym at all."

She shrugs and points out, "There's not much else to do."

"We could just drink in the den?" I offer, grasping at a way to make it more acceptable. Carter knows I go to the den, so if Addison happened to come in there, he couldn't blame me for that. Well, he could. He'll probably find some way to stop it from happening as it is.

"That sounds perfect," she tells me with a broad smile. Daniel drags her away just as the timer goes off on the stove.

With a genuine smile and a short wave, she says sweetly, "I'll see you tomorrow."

It's kind of her, but I have no idea if I will.

Seeing how blind she is to everything, I'm reminded of how little I knew in my father's house. Even being oblivious to everything else, she still has a sad smile. I guess there's not much difference between knowing the truth and being blind to it. The effect is still the same.

CHAPTER 20

Carter

SHE'S SO LOST, my Aria. I can't take my eyes from her as she stares at the comforter, her fingertips barely grazing it before she pulls the sheets back. Her expression is a mix of emotions. Sadness, confusion, the barest hint of anger. As the seconds pass, her chest flushes, and the lust of knowing what's to come takes over. But her brow stays furrowed as the bed groans with her small weight and the sheets rustle.

I don't think for a second that she's gotten over her anger, but it's not as raw as it was hours ago, let alone where she was yesterday. I still don't know what set her off at the front door, but I'm going to find out. She can't hide from me forever and I don't buy that bullshit that there was nothing in particular. I watched the surveillance cameras over and over again. Something happened. I just don't know what.

I loosen my watchband, feeling the slick metal brush against my wrist before placing it back in its spot in the drawer. My gaze is still pinned on Aria, who's looking anywhere but back at me, her fingers fiddling with her necklace. Another second, another heavy breath.

The internal war is waning, but war leaves casualties, and I know she's taking record of everything she's lost and what's left of the woman she once was. I watch as she swallows, her chest rising higher and her breathing quickening.

She's so close to submitting everything to me. So, fucking close.

She doesn't even see it.

"You can't stay mad at me forever," I tell her as I pull my shirt over my head, grabbing it by the back of the collar.

I kick off my pants and ready myself to join her in bed, wondering if she'll tense when I wrap my arms around her. It's only fair that it guts me every night when she does it. I'm more than certain I deserve a harsher punishment.

"Do you know Addison spoke to me today?" she asks me with an edge of anxiousness rather than acknowledging what I've said. She doesn't seem to have taken my confession in the den earlier to heart, but she's more guarded now than she was before. Maybe she doesn't remember, but I thought it would change something between us. For the better.

My lips twitch with the hint of a feigned smile. "I do," I tell her, and she finally looks at me with a pleading expression.

"And?" she asks with clear curiosity but the desperation weighing heavier.

"And what?" I ask her as if I can't comprehend her line of questioning. Addison knows who I am, and I agree this situation is less than moral, but if she were to learn the truth, she would still love my brother. She'd still be family. She'll forgive me. Daniel's sins have been substantial, and she's forgiven him, mostly.

"Are you going to let me go?"

Her bottom lip wavers, but she waits patiently as I drop my hand to hers, thinking carefully about my next words.

"You'll like Addison," I tell her genuinely. "I won't stop you, and I won't be there to control you; I don't have any interest in it either."

"So, you don't care?" she questions.

"I care, but not in the way you think. Why would I want to stop you two from getting to know one another?" I ask her and then add, "My brother won't either. You two should get to know each other." I don't let on how anxious I am to hear what she tells Addison and whether or not she confides in her.

"I could tell her you're holding me hostage, that you trapped me in a cell for weeks…" she answers me with a cocked brow although she can't hide the sadness that still lingers in her expression. I can see so clearly that the very idea of how we became what we are now, tortures her.

"Would you really want to bring her into this?" I ask her pointedly. "She's having a hard time, and you and I both know she wouldn't react well to that."

"What if I say something I shouldn't?" she whispers quietly with genuine concern. I watch as she picks at the blanket, clearly on edge with the prospect of saying something that would cause more problems for our already delicate situation.

"Don't," is the only answer I have for her. "Be careful with what you say."

The silence stretches for a moment and I consider her.

"Maybe it's best you forget all this for a moment, and just talk to her as you would have anyone else a month ago."

I have to be so delicate with her. Ever so delicate. She doesn't answer, although the careful tiptoeing around her words slips away as she adjusts under the covers.

"We have other matters to discuss," I tell her as my thumb runs along the stubble of my jaw.

Although she nods, a heavy sigh leaves her in a staggering way, the sleep showing in her expression. She's overwhelmed and exhausted. Neither of us slept last night. Even after crying half the night, she woke every hour.

"What happened yesterday can't happen again. You have a choice. You can take your punishment now, or you can have it after your date with Addison."

Her body tenses and she struggles to form words,

her lips parting and strangled breaths taking the place of whatever her question is.

"You won't be sending me back to the cell then?" she finally asks, her voice as strained as her body is stiff.

"That wouldn't do you any good." I wrap my arm around her, comforting her and leave a small kiss on the crown of her head. I whisper, "I told you, you shouldn't be left alone. This punishment is to benefit us. I promise you that," I tell her and feel the weight of everything looming in my thoughts.

I can see her swallowing her words. Practically reading her mind, I can see how she wants to tell me that we would be better if I would let this war go or let her go, but she doesn't dare speak it.

"What is it?" she asks me.

"I haven't decided yet," I tell her honestly.

"Tomorrow then," she tells me softly with defeat in her expression and it shreds me, but tomorrow she'll see.

"Is this what it will always be like?" she asks. "I do something you don't like, and I'm punished for it and then fucked until I forget I hate you?"

I don't think she meant her question to be humorous, but a short chuckle makes my chest shake. Running my fingers down her arm, I decide to tell her more, to set boundaries. But with them comes new rules.

"In the bedroom, I want you to obey. Anywhere else," my blood pumps harder and hotter as I finish, "I want you as mine."

"There's a difference?" she asks with feigned sarcasm. That mouth of hers is going to get her in trouble. Her disobedience shouldn't make me as hard as it does. As much as I love it, tomorrow night she'll be punished. There's no mistaking that.

"You already know there is," I say and although my voice comes out deep and foreboding, I try to lighten it. "It's time for a new game, Aria."

"No games." Her voice rises, and she has to lower it before adding, "I'm done playing games with you, Carter."

"You'll never be done with me." My words whisper against her skin. "You already know that."

Her fingernails dig into the sheets, pulling them tighter as she continues to avoid looking at me. I know why she doesn't want to meet my heated gaze. It will make hers fill with desire, too. She can't deny what she feels for me and how much power is in the tension between us. The push and pull that drives me wild does the same for her. The difference is that I can admit it; even if it will destroy me, I can fucking admit what she does to me.

"What do you want?" she asks me although she stares straight ahead, her expression flat and indifferent. "Tell me what you want from me," she says, and a spike of anger plays in her tone. "Tell me what it means to be yours," she asks through clenched teeth and I merely stare back at her. She already knows. We both know that she knows exactly what it means.

"Here you fuck me... you punish me like you did before." I don't miss how her eyes darken as she gazes around the room, looking to where I've spanked her, throat fucked her, made her cum harder than she ever had before.

"Yes," I tell her and watch as her pupils dilate and her legs scissor to ease some of the heat growing between her legs.

"And what do you expect outside of this room?" she asks and when she does, her voice wavers. She knows how much is at stake.

"For them to fear you." Her eyes flash to mine and suddenly my songbird is very much interested. I continue, "The way they fear me."

She laughs a sad and pathetic sound, ripping her gaze from me as she shakes her head. Her soft lips part, but no words come out and instead, she continues to shake her head and stares at the knob of the bathroom door across the room. Looking anywhere but at me.

"Fear is easy to attain," I tell her the simple fact. And it truly is. Keeping it is the curse that never fades. But I can bear the weight of that burden. She only needs to play the part. They have to believe it.

She shakes her head gently as if I don't understand. She tells me, "I want to draw. Maybe own a studio one day. That's my ambition. Or sell some of my pieces to people who would love them the way I do. I want them to feel what I feel when they look at them." I can see the light of hope in her eyes as she tells me a dream of hers I would never have known otherwise. I can give her that, so easily. All she had to do was tell me. "That's the only thing I've ever wanted beyond being happy. Having a family and making them happy."

A family.

I can give her that too, and the thought of her swollen with my child makes me force back a groan of want in my throat. Closing my eyes, I remind myself she needs time. All in good time. Once the war is over, everything will change.

Opening my eyes, I ask her, "And what does any of that have to do with what I've asked of you?" My question catches her off guard. "You forget the world you live in." A family, a gallery. It's all so easily attainable. But only when we have control. And that requires fear. They *must* fear her.

I ask her, "You want that studio? A gallery? Children, Aria? Do you think your name alone is one that wouldn't put a target on your back?" She flinches at the question and I can see the doubt and worry play across her face. Her lips turn down as her breathing picks up. It doesn't matter if Aria stands beside me or not; the minute she was given the name Talvery, her entire life was at risk.

"Anything that gives you pride or happiness is a weakness waiting to be exploited. But only if anyone would dare to cross you. And Aria, if you haven't noticed, the stunt I pulled the other night will lead to whispers of what you mean to me. And that makes you a far greater weakness to exploit than you ever were to your father."

"So, that's what I am? A weakness?"

The tension grows between us as her expression softens but stays riddled with curiosity. She whispers a question I know has been torturing her. I watch her soft lips as she asks, "What do I mean to you? *Me.* Not the girl you thought I was."

I replay her words that one of her greatest ambitions was to make her family happy, feeling my heartbeat slow as if time is forced to pause for me to consider how to answer her.

The mere idea of ensuring her happiness is becoming a greater ambition to me than anything else has ever been. If I spoke those words to her now, she'd laugh in my face. She doesn't see what I see. She doesn't know what I know. I could never tell her. I don't have the words even if she was ready for them.

She doesn't have the forgiveness to offer me for what I've put her through and what I'm going to put her through.

She wouldn't believe me if I told her this is for her. That it's all for her. And if she did, she'd still use it against me. She doesn't even realize the woman she can be. The defiance and stubbornness that makes her perfection in my eyes.

"I'll show you what you mean to me, Aria." My voice is rough and deep but holds nothing but sincerity. "Until then, the new game has started. This room is for fucking you, punishing you and giving you pleasure beyond imagine. And outside of this room, you will be mine, and you will demand respect and earn the fear that's owed to you."

Her hazel-green eyes brim with something I've yet to see.

"Carter Cross," she whispers my name. "I don't know that I'm the woman you think I am." Her words are etched with sorrow as if she really believes what she says.

I lean in closer to her, resting my lips against her shoulder and running the tip of my nose along her skin. My lips caress her jaw where I kiss her gently and then nip the lobe of her ear.

I whisper along the shell of her ear, watching goosebumps form down her shoulder and across her chest, pebbling her nipples. "You have so much to learn and so much to accept, but Aria," I open my eyes to stare into hers before I continue, "I know you won't disappoint me."

My gaze focused on her lips, I speak more to myself than to her, "It's all been leading to this."

CHAPTER 21

Aria

I HAVE three hours and a single bottle of wine. I should've grabbed a second bottle, knowing Carter will be waiting for me in his bedroom when this rendezvous is over.

There's a tension in my chest, a faint flicker of life in my heart with the nerves of what's waiting for me.

The idea of running back to the hideaway room flutters into my mind every so often. Carter held up his word that he wouldn't come for me the first time I fled there, but what are the odds he'll do that again? If I try to avoid the punishment and him, I have a feeling everything will only get worse. There's a single distraction I'm grateful for though. Someone to talk to and someone who doesn't know what I'm going through.

I'm indebted to Addison, even if she has no idea. In fact, I'm grateful she has no idea.

Popping the cork out of the bottle, I stop pretending as if hiding will do anything at all. I may fear Carter at times, along with the thoughts of punishment, but there's a darker piece of my soul that craves it.

I can't deny the idea of being throat fucked or tied up by the most powerful man I've ever met has every nerve ending in my body lit like a fuse waiting to go off.

Even as I pour the wine, listening to the sound of it, I think of every way Carter's punished me before. How hot and eager he made me for more as he played my body against my emotions. Even still, I'm numb with grief.

It makes no sense. Save the fact that my heart is truly torn and in disarray.

The dark liquid swirls as I set the bottle down and lift my glass to my lips, breathing in the dark blend to fill my lungs. Maybe I've truly lost it all. Maybe I'm crazy at this point.

I need something to give. Everything is about to fall apart in front of my eyes and just out of reach. But how do I change any of it? What I truly need is mercy from a heartless man dead set on revenge.

"There you are," I hear Addison before I see her and my heart attempts to leap up my throat, beating chaotically as if caught in an unspeakable act.

"Hey," I breathe out and my voice wavers. The wine

in my glass swishes from being jostled and to steady it, I hold the stem with both hands.

"This kind of feels like a blind date, doesn't it?" Addison jokes with a genuine smile. Her mood is greatly improved from yesterday. She almost seems like a different person from what I've seen before.

Carefree and excited. There's a sweetness about her and the air around her as she walks into the room. Without hesitation, she picks up a glass and fills it.

"It kind of does," I agree with a dry laugh and a half-smile and the awkwardness wanes. My hands are clammy as she lifts up her glass for a cheers and I do the same.

"To new friends." She tilts her head with the same smile on her lips, but it's softer as the glass clinks.

Sighing, she settles into the sofa, making herself comfortable. "I've only been in this room the one time," Addison starts talking although she's not looking at me at all. She tucks her legs up under her as she sets the glass down on the end table and stares at a black and white photograph framed just to the right of the mantel. "Carter wanted to show me he'd hung my pictures," she says softly and then glances at me. "I think he just wanted to make me smile and feel welcomed, you know?"

My brow raises in surprise. "These are yours?" I ask her, finding the conversation a wonderful distraction for the well of emotion that constantly pulls me into the tide of depression I've been feeling. The idea of Carter doing anything for her just to make her happy has questions drifting in the forefront of my mind, but

I swat them away. No thoughts of Carter or anything else. I've proven to myself I'm incapable of processing it all.

Every few minutes, my mood has changed today. Whether I think of Nikolai and his impending execution, my father and what he did to Carter and the Cross brothers, the fact that he hasn't come for me, or Carter himself and the cruel things he says and the murders he has planned.

Yet the prospect of falling into his arms for him to soothe all the painful twists and turns this week has given me, somehow clouds my judgment and that's where I want to stay. Accepting a comfort and turning my back on reality.

Maybe that's why I'm growing to hate myself. Yes, I truly think I'm going insane. And I'd blame Carter if only I could remember what he's done and what he plans to do when he kisses me and takes all the pain away.

"All of them but those two," she says and points out two abstract watercolor paintings behind us that straddle the entrance to the den. Tugging my skirt down, I clear my throat and smile. The kind of smile I've given others before when I know that's what they expect to see.

Sometimes that smile turns into a genuine one, and that's what I hope this turns into. I pray that's what it will be.

"You're very talented." I have to admire her work yet again. It's not the first time I've noticed them. "They're stunning."

Her fair features blush and her shoulders dip a little as she waves me away and jokingly says, "Aw shucks," causing me to let out a gentle laugh. "That's kind of you."

"I love art," I tell her and for some reason the generic statement makes me scrunch up my nose. "I love the ones that make you feel." My hands gesture in the air toward my chest to make my point. "Like with yours." My words fail me, and I have to close my eyes, shaking my head for a moment, so I can put the right words in order to get out exactly what I mean. "It seems so simple, even with the black and white taking away even more of what we'd see normally. But in the simplicity, there's so much more there that speaks to a raw side of your soul like you can feel what the photographer feels, or any artist by focusing on an object that would have such little meaning if you saw it in passing. In the art, it begs to tell you a story and you can already feel what the story is about."

"I knew you were a girl of my own heart," Addison says and offers me a kind smile. "I have to admit," she leans forward, hushing her voice, "I've seen your drawings and I could say the same right back to you."

"Thank you," I tell her, feeling the happiness of a shared interest, but also realizing the ice has been broken and the questions she has for me are probably similar to the ones I have for her. The questions beg to slip through and bring me back to the train of thought I was on moments ago.

It's too easy to just be friendly, to sit on the surface

of the world we live in and pretend that everything is just fine.

"So where are you from?" Addison asks me, taking another sip, her lips already staining from the wine, and then she reaches for the throw blanket. I finally take a seat on the armchair I've been leaning against. The leather groans as I sink down in it and sit cross-legged to be comfortable.

"Close to here," I tell her and ignore how my heart beats harder, my fingers tracing along my ankle to keep them busy while I carefully avoid details. I can't look her in the eyes as I wonder if she knows where I come from and who my family is. My throat dries but before it can cause my words to crack, I quickly ask her, "What about you?"

Glancing at her, I can feel the anxiety course harder in my veins, but her expression stays casual and easy. I get the impression that Addison is more laidback than I am. Harder to shake. Stronger in a lot of ways. And for some reason, that thought weighs against my chest heavily as she answers.

"I grew up around here, but left and traveled for the past, like five years, almost six years now?" Her voice is light as she continues. "I've lived all over."

"That's amazing," I say with wonder. I've never left home. I've never ventured outside of the parameters I was given.

"Did you live on your own?"

Addison nods with a sly grin and then clucks her tongue. "I was kind of running away at first," she says, and her voice is lower as she shrugs and then takes a heavy gulp of wine. She licks her lower lip and stares at the glass as she says, "It was too hard to stay." She peeks up at me and her piercing green eyes stay with mine as she says, "It was far too easy to just keep going, you know? Rather than staying still and having to deal with it all."

The jealousy I felt only moments ago instantly turns to compassion. Her tone is too raw, too open, and honest not to feel the pain of her confession.

"Yeah, I get that," I tell her and settle deeper into the seat. "I really do."

Time passes quietly as I slowly pick through the questions, one that won't open up a raw wound unless she cares to go there herself. "What brought you back?" I ask.

"Daniel." She rolls her eyes as she says his name, but she can't hide how her smile grows, how her cheeks flush and she pulls her legs into herself as if his name's only home is on her lips. "We bumped into each other a few towns over and he brought me back."

My smile matches hers as she continues her story. "We grew up together—kind of. I kind of grew up with him and his brothers I guess. It's a complicated story," she says then waves me off, wine glass in her hand, although she takes a long minute before sipping it again, staring past me at the mantel.

"This one is delicious," she says before finishing it off.

"I love the dark reds." My statement is spoken as absently as she spoke hers.

"They're the best," she says wide-eyed and then reaches for the bottle for another glass.

"You two getting along all right?" Daniel's voice carries through the den before he's even taken a step into the room.

My skin pricks with unease, being brought back to reality when I'd been slipping into a hiding place of Addison's story. I keep my smile plastered on my face as he glances between the two of us.

I wonder if he thinks I'd tell her why I'm here and what happened. That I'd warn her away from Daniel and expose that he knew. That I'd beg her to help me and frighten her.

My heart feels like it collapses in on itself as the two of them go back and forth in lighthearted banter although a touch of tension is obvious.

"Always hovering," Addison says although there's a quiet reverence there that Daniel doesn't seem to grasp. He sighs and runs his hand down the back of his head before saying, "I just came to see if you two needed anything."

Addison playfully slaps his arm as he stops behind the sofa where she's sitting. "Liar. You came to eavesdrop."

"You got me," he says and lets her shoo him away with a simple, "Get out," but not without a kiss.

Addison lifts from her seat, making the blanket around her waist fall as her ass lifts up. "Love you," she whispers and then gives him a peck. Then another and another. Three in quick succession.

With the tip of his nose brushing against hers he says with his eyes closed, "Love you too."

And there isn't an ounce of me that doesn't believe them both. My smile falls and there's no way I could fake one in this moment. Love exists in their exchange; it breathes in the air between them.

It's undeniable and nothing like what binds me to Carter. It's not lust, it's a meeting of souls, the two of them needing one another and recognizing that truth.

"You need anything?" Daniel asks again as my gaze drifts to the side table. The edge of the carved wood grants me a small escape from their display.

"Aria," Daniel's voice is raised as he addresses me directly. "You need anything?" he asks me, and his eyes carry his real question, *Are you okay?*

"I'm fine," I tell him as evenly as I can and then clear my throat before reaching for my glass again.

It takes a long moment after he's left for the tense air to change.

"So, you and Carter?" Addison asks me, cocking a brow to be comical. She sips the wine but keeps her eyes on me and the expression on her face makes me laugh.

"Yeah, me and Carter," I tell her tightly, but with humor.

"He's keeping you trapped here too, huh?" she asks and the easy interaction that existed before turns sharp.

"You could say that," I reply but my voice is flat. Chewing on the inside of my cheek, I consider telling her the truth for a split second, but there's no way I ever would. Not because I don't trust her, but because I'm truly ashamed in this moment.

I've given up. I'm lying in bed with the devil. And as much as Addison appears to like me, there's no way she'd ever respect me if she knew the truth. I don't even respect myself.

"I'm guessing he chased you?" she asks speculatively. "The Cross boys tend to chase."

"Again, you could say that."

"When I first I met Carter," Addison starts to tell me a story, realizing I'm not open to sharing my own Carter tale, while her thin finger drifts over the edge of the wine glass, running circles around the rim of it. "He was different from the other brothers."

"How so?" I ask, watching her finger as my shame eases.

She glances at me for a moment with a pinched expression. "He wasn't around as often, and he was always quiet when he was around, but you knew the moment he was in the house. He *was* the authority."

"What do you mean?"

"Like their father wasn't the best, you know? After their mother died, he took it really hard." She swallows as if a painful memory threatened to choke her if she continued, but she goes on. "So, if anyone needed anything, it was Carter who was asked. Carter who made the rules. Carter who got whatever was needed."

I watch her expression as she tells me their story.

"This one time, it was so stupid." Her eyes get glassy but she shakes her head and brushes her hair back.

"These kids stole our bikes," she tells me, forcing strength to her voice.

"Tyler took me to the corner store and we left our bikes outside, and these assholes stole them." She laughs the kind of laugh that you force out when you want a release from the need to cry.

"You knew Tyler?" I ask her, feeling a chill run down my skin, leaving goosebumps along their path. Nikolai told me once that when you have that feeling run through you, it means someone's walked over your grave.

She only nods, her eyes reflecting a sad secret, and then continues. "It had to be these guys, they were older and there were like six of them. Grown ass men who had nothing better to do than steal bikes from high school kids." She breathes in deeply before smoothing the blanket down across her lap and telling me, "We walked home and the last ten minutes it rained the whole way. We were soaked when we got back."

"Daniel wasn't there; Tyler went to him first because he didn't like to bother Carter. None of the boys ever liked to bother him with petty stuff, you know?" she asks me, and I don't know how to respond but she doesn't give me time to regardless.

"So, Carter was there and asked what happened. He was quick to anger back then, so much different from now," she tells me, and I look at her as if she's crazy, but she doesn't see. She picks at the blanket and continues. "He and Tyler left together in the truck, Carter told me to stay back and within hours, both bikes were in the back of the truck safe at home. Tyler was never one to fight. He was a lover and a kind old soul, but he said those guys wouldn't mess with us anymore. I kind of wish I'd seen what Carter had done." She says the last words like a spoken thought that had just come to her. All I can think is that she's probably better off not having witnessed what Carter did to those men.

"I guess that's not the best story," she says and shrugs. "Sorry, I kind of suck at telling stories."

I offer her a soft smile and say, "I liked it."

"Anyway, that's what Carter does. He takes what he wants and doesn't take any prisoners or put up with any bullshit."

Her words strike me in a way I can't explain and the same tears that she'd wiped away haphazardly at the start of her story, threaten to fall from mine.

"Are you okay?" she asks me, although judging by the way her smile wavers, I could ask her the same.

My lips part ready to do what I've always done, to tell everyone that I'm fine. To pretend like nothing's wrong.

"Only if you want to talk," she quickly adds, practically tripping over her words. Even her hands come up in protest. "I'm not usually this weird, I've just been on edge lately and it's so nice to be able to talk to someone else. Someone who's not...," she stops and holds her breath, searching for the right words but none come. I can see it in her eyes that she's suffering like I am. Something's wrong and I can only guess that it's because she's trapped here. Trapped like I am, but for such different reasons.

"I'm okay, and I get it… I do." My attempt to reassure her falls flat. She offers me a weak half smile that doesn't reach her eyes.

"I wish I could tell you something," she whispers and then shakes her head as if she's losing her mind. Maybe I'm not the only crazy one in this room. Wiping under her eyes she looks to the door and exhales a harsh breath. "I should go." Maybe she had a curfew time too. Or maybe she just doesn't want to break down in front of a stranger.

Glancing at the clock, I see nearly three hours has already passed. I feel like we've only just sat down.

"Yeah, I should too." I clear my throat and try to think of something to say that's comforting for her even though I hardly know her. A piece of her though, her heart and soul, I know well. "I'm here if you ever want a drinking buddy," I offer.

"Or to binge-watch something good on Netflix?" she offers, and the genuine happiness lights up her expression.

"Sure," I offer her a smile with my upturned voice and imagine the loss I can already feel doesn't exist.

"This might sound weird," Addison tells me as she picks up her wine glass and downs the last remaining bit before looking me in the eyes, "but you look like you could use 'a somebody.'" She sets the glass down, the clinking of the glass breaking up the white noise that drowns me when Addison stares down at me, standing up on her way to leave. She pushes the hair off of her shoulder and tells me solemnly, "I didn't have 'a somebody' for a long time. And I know how it feels."

It's hard to describe the pain and hollowness of having a stranger seem to see through you and when they look there, they want to help you, to be there for you with a genuine kindness. When you look back at them, you see it too. It's so obvious but speaking the truth would make it real, and it's so much more comforting to run and hide or pretend like everything is okay for at least a little while.

I have to clear my dry, scratchy throat before I tell her, "I might take you up on that."

CHAPTER 22

Carter

THE FLOOR CREAKING alerts me to her coming. The bathroom light is still on and the soft yellow light filters into the room, casting a shadow where she stands. Aria's never looked so tempting and radiant. Licking her lips in defiance even though there's fear and defeat in her gorgeous hazel eyes. Naked, with her skin flushed from the prospect of what's coming, she stands there caught in my gaze.

I've never been so hard in my fucking life. I know she needs this. We both need it. The last few days have been large steps back with only meager steps forward.

She stands before me as my equal, daring, and relentless, although on the opposite side from where I stand.

"Come," I command her as I sit on the chair and run my hand down my right thigh.

She walks in from the bathroom hesitantly, her body stiff but still she comes to me, stopping in front of me and waiting.

"Sit," I tell her, and she instinctively reaches for my hand as I pull her ass down to nestle in my crotch. She stiffens her back and continues to pretend she doesn't need this. She knows better if only she'd open her eyes.

"I've thought a lot about what's causing tension between us." The statement comes out deep and husky, unable to deny my desire for her. I let my middle finger slip along her shoulder and watch as it makes her nipples pebble. Her beautiful skin both flushes and at the same time pricks with goosebumps.

"The first thing I'm going to do is punish you." Her lips part with a quick breath, but she nods her head in understanding. "The second is to give you something you want, and something you need..." I pause my movement and wait for her beautiful hazel-green gaze to meet mine before adding, "If you take the punishment well."

Her breathing quickens, and I can see how her blood pumps harder in the veins of her neck but still, she nods in obedience. Her eyes continue to flicker to mine with questions, but she doesn't ask them.

"Lie across my lap," I tell her gently. There's no need to be firm, knowing what's to come. Nervously, she obeys but tries to hold on to the chair as her balance is off and her legs dangle aimlessly.

I adjust her, so she's positioned perfectly, her hip on

my right thigh and she gasps in protest, but it's short-lived.

"Hands behind your back," I command her, and she obeys, although she's awkward in my lap, trying to balance herself. It doesn't matter though, the second I grip both her wrists in my left hand and press them to the small of her back, she's steady. And that's how she'll stay until I decide this punishment is over. Her pussy is already glistening; the mix of fear and desire is a powerful thing.

My blunt fingernails trail over her pale, supple ass as I give her a simple command. "Tell me why you ran from me when I gave you access to the front door." My chest feels tight with worry that she'll never see. I won't allow her to question my control. Not again. Never again. She needs to know in every fiber of her being, that I can take control from her but that more than that, she needs it.

"I need to know what set you off, Aria," I say clearly enough to be sure she understands how much this means to me when she doesn't answer.

"I don't know," she tells me with a tense voice before blowing a strand of hair out of her face.

The lying will come to an end shortly.

Slap! My hand stings all the way down to my wrist as the bright mark lands on her right cheek and Aria cries out, her hips bucking uselessly as I hold her down with a firm grip and do the same to her other cheek. Moving to her center, I slap her there and then again on the right cheek. All the while, she writhes in my lap and cries out with muffled screams of protest.

My heart hammers and my dick hardens when my fingers drift lower to her cunt. Her breathing hitches, and her entrance clenches around my fingertips but she gets no reward for lying to me.

I speak softly as I gently lay my hand on her hot cheek, rubbing soothing strokes over the sensitized marks. "Tell me the truth." My command falls into the silence that mixes with her strangled moans as the pain and pleasure combine. I dip my fingers to her cunt, letting them run through her slick folds. My middle finger trails down to her clit and I circle it once, tempting her and rewarding her obedience as she stays where she is, where she belongs on my lap. "Tell me, Aria."

With a shaky breath, Aria's back attempts to bow and her thighs clench. She visibly swallows, and I know she's going to cum, so I stop. My finger is still pressed against her, but without the movement, she lifts her eyes to mine, breathing heavily with her lips parted.

"I don't know," she answers, her mesmerizing hazel eyes begging me to believe her. I don't wait for her to prepare. I spank her other cheek and then move back to the right before returning to the left repeatedly, feeling a burn that runs up my arm as my hand goes numb.

Aria's scream echoes in the room as her body stiffens across my lap. She seethes, sucking in air through clenched teeth as tears prick her eyes. My own breathing rages from me as I land the last blow and keep her steady where she is.

Gulping for breath and hanging her head low while

attempting to fight the need to struggle against the hold I have on her, she turns her head away from me. But I see the tears.

Instantly, I place my hand over her heated skin, ignoring how she jumps and applying enough pressure to soothe the pain. My heart skips once, then twice as she struggles to maintain her composure, the tears falling freely as her face reddens.

"I've got you," I whisper to her and she turns to glance up at me, a look of pure hate on her expression. "Tell me what happened, and it stops," I offer her again, and watch as her bottom lip wavers. "I won't let you go until you tell me."

Her face crumples and she sobs out, "It's stupid," before letting the tears fall again.

I continue rubbing soothing circles, occasionally squeezing her ass to keep the blood flowing and the nerve endings on edge. The endorphins flowing in her blood will make her pleasure that much greater. Both the body and mind always prefer pleasure to pain.

And I'll give her both. Although she hates me now, she'll love me when this is over.

My fingers drift to her core this time, pressing inside of her and I'm instantly rewarded with her arching her neck, her eyes closed as a small moan of pleasure drifts from her reddened lips. Her cheeks are tearstained, and a few droplets still linger on her lashes.

Her cunt clamps around my fingertips, begging me for more.

A strangled moan fills the hot air as my cock hardens even more and presses against her belly. Fuck,

I want her. I *need* to have her tonight and claim her again. To remind her of how much she belongs with me.

"Tell me now, Aria," I demand, my voice deep and rumbling with the need I feel alive in every cell of my body.

She only whimpers, and then defiantly shakes her head. "I don't know, I swear I--"

Before she can even finish, I slap her ass as hard as I can. The pain that had numbed brightens back to life. Under her ass cheeks, on her ass, on her pussy. I spank her in a new spot each time, rotating between them but the pace is ruthless, the slaps unforgiving. My jaw clenches and the pain rips up my arm as she screams out.

"Stop lying to me," I barely get the command out through clenched teeth as I stop the punishment, forcing myself to breathe and instantly soothe her reddened skin.

She heaves in a breath and then another. A shudder runs down her body that morphs her sobs to moans. She's close to this being so much more. But what I want are answers and she won't cum until I get them. I'll make damn sure of that.

The hair on the side of her face, wet from her tears, is stuck to her skin as she says, "I saw the date."

Her upper body rocks and she tries to move away from me, groaning with a pained expression before telling me, "I saw the date on your phone." Her words are spastic at best, but I know I heard her right.

My breathing is still erratic, my hand stinging with

pain and my lungs refusing to move as I take in what she's telling me.

My fingers loosen on her wrists slowly as I wrap my arm around her waist, careful not to touch her ass until I'm ready to set her on my lap.

She winces and seethes, not moving her arms even though she freely could.

Bringing her into my chest, I let her collapse in my arms. Her hands lift to my shoulders as the tears soak into my shirt. The feel of her cheek on my shoulder as she buries her head in the crook of my neck is already a soothing balm to me.

"You saw the date?" I prompt her to tell me more. To explain it to me as I comfort her.

"The day before was my mother's--" she gasps, not finishing and I run my hand up and down her back, letting her cling to me.

I shush her, letting my warm breath whisper along her hair and I wait for her to settle.

"You missed the anniversary of your mother's death?" I ask her, feeling a pain inside me crumple every bit of strength I have.

"Yes," she croaks and tries to climb closer to me as if she wasn't already pressed against me. "It was the first time," she says in between breaths, "that I didn't go to her grave."

Holding her while she cries, knowing the pain she's feeling could have been avoided so easily. I could have done something to help her, even if it meant gathering dozens of men to protect her while she saw to her mother's grave. I could have done something if only I'd known.

"I'm sorry." I try to put every ounce of compassion into my apology. "Please believe how sorry I am," I say and kiss her hair, her shoulder and then pull her away to kiss her swollen red lips.

She buries herself back into the crook of my neck and then cries out as her ass brushes against my pants.

"Thank you for telling me," I say as I maneuver her on my lap, so I have access to her cunt. "Hold on to me," I command her, and she does instantly. She needs someone to hold and someone to hold her, I've never been more sure of it.

"This will make the pain go away," I tell her, although my words are hollow. Pleasure can hide only one specific kind of pain. I rub her clit first, letting the intensity from the unique pleasure that comes after both pain and mourning flow through her.

She bites down on my shoulder, her fingernails digging into my skin through my shirt. She writhes on my lap, so close to the edge already, although each time her ass brushes against the fabric of my pants, her voice hitches, and her grip on me tightens.

Pressing my fingers inside her, I stroke her ruthlessly and butt my palm against her clit. Her back bows and I have to hold her closer to me, laying my hand against her shoulder.

"Cum for me," I whisper in her ear. My cock is hard and desperate to be wrapped in her hot cunt, but I can't take my pleasure from her like this.

It's all for her.

"Carter," she gasps my name as her body rocks with pleasure and her head falls back. I don't stop until she's trembling, and her cries have stopped completely.

My heart races against hers, sweat covering my skin and every muscle in my body coiled.

Time passes slowly as I wait until she's calm and coherent. And each second, I carefully select the words she needs to hear.

With weak balance, she finally lifts her head to look me in the eyes. Her expression pinches as she leans back, feeling her raw ass brush against my pants once again, but this time her lips part and another orgasm threatens from the faint touch.

"I need more from you," I tell her, breaking her moment and forcing her hazel eyes to stare into mine.

"I have you here," I say as I let my fingers fall to her pussy and then cup it, watching as she gasps, throwing her head back and rocking herself into my hand. My lips drop to her throat, whispering against her skin, "So needy."

Before she can get off again, I stop and wait for her eyes to reach mine, dark with desire and lit with lust. "I'm getting to you here," I tell her and smooth her hair back on the crown of her head.

A moment passes with a tense beating in my chest before I drop my fingers to her chest, between her bare breasts and ask her, "What about here?"

My eyes flicker between where I'm touching her and her own gaze, now swirling with a hopelessness and sadness I wish I could take away.

The ever-present vise tightens on my heart as she

asks me in a whisper, "If I gave you that, what would I have left?"

It tightens further, and my heart refuses to beat. The answer is so obvious. "You'd have me." I watch her expression remain unchanged and I have to look away.

Breathing in deeply, I ignore whatever I'm feeling, every last bit of it, knowing logically, she's close. I know she is.

She comes and goes, and that's because of her father. If he wasn't in the picture, she would be mine completely. And Nikolai...

"You know what I need, Carter," Aria finally speaks and when she does her voice cracks. Tears linger in her eyes. "For you to have my heart, you can't destroy it. You can't kill them."

I cave. Knowing what this could be, I offer her something, just to have a chance to break through the wall that guards her heart. "I'll call him, but you'll be silent."

With a look of shock and gratitude, she leans in closer to me and starts to speak but I press my finger against her lips, silencing her and halting her movements.

Fear is power. And every day, I fear her never loving me more than the day before. I've given her the power and I don't know how I let that happen.

"I will call your father and you'll listen only. Is that clear?"

Although she nods, she doesn't speak until I move my finger away. "Yes, Carter."

It occurs to me how little she obeys unless she has

hope. I instantly regret telling her I would call her prick of a father.

I need to give her hope in something else. Because when this war is over, her father will be dead, and she'll have to find forgiveness or be miserable and hate me forever.

CHAPTER 23

Aria

I DON'T KNOW how I slept at all.

I keep wondering if he's really going to do it. If Carter is going to call my father and if he does, what would he say? I almost ask Carter if I can call Nikolai, just to tell him I'm safe but I don't know how Carter would react, and I don't want to push him when he's given me this hope.

If my father knew Carter gave me Stephan to kill, literally forced to stay put with a knife placed in my hand, wouldn't that offer some sort of truce between them?

My hands are shaking so much from the anticipation and anxiety of what they'll say that the picture in front of me is blank, not from lack of inspiration, but from the inability to create even a simple line.

An hour has passed with me sitting on the floor of Carter's office, listening to the tapping of keys and the steady tick-tock of the clock. All the while, I can't focus on anything. Not a damn thing except for when Carter's going to call him like he said he would.

Glancing up at Carter, I catch his gaze and I know the look in my eyes is pleading and expectant.

"You need more." Carter's voice is deep and low, and it booms through the office. Or, maybe it's just that I'm on high alert and everything is thrumming to life as I wait for what's to come.

My throat tightens, feeling the dejection once again for the one thing that could change everything, but I stand on shaking legs and go to him.

It doesn't escape me that he has me under control again. That my only desire is to obey him, so he'll give me what he claimed he would. He may have given me false hope.

My heart flickers like a candle so close to its flame going out. He wouldn't do that to me. I refuse to believe it. I know he feels something for me. He must. I can feel it in the very marrow of my bones.

Carter pushes the phone farther away from him, an old desk phone, and I stare at it as I hear him push the laptop and stacks of papers out of the way.

It's right there. *Just call him.*

Pat, pat, he pats the top of the desk and I take the hint, lying on my belly, knowing he's going to lift the dark red chiffon dress up my thighs and bare my backside to him.

My cheek presses against the hard desk and I can feel my heart hammer against it. Gripping on to the edge of the desk, I wait for the cool gel to hit my sore ass. There aren't any bruises this time, but somehow it hurts more. This morning I nearly cried waking up to the pain until Carter used the ointment.

Sucking in a deep breath, my eyes close and I feel Carter rub the soothing balm into my hot skin. It's tender still, but even more so, it makes me crave more of his touch.

A soft hum of gratitude and want leaves my lips, and it's met with a rough chuckle from Carter. Opening my eyes, I glance up at him, although I have to push the lock of hair out of my face.

My heart does that flickering again.

"It looks much better than how it was last night and this morning."

"It feels better now too," I tell him easily, watching his expression as he pays close attention to where he's rubbing the balm.

"You didn't tell me the entire truth last night," Carter says before opening a drawer and then closing it. My heart thumps once, thinking of what I left out but having nothing come to mind.

I don't know if he just put the gel back or if he's taken something else out.

Before I can answer, Carter tells me, "You forgot to mention your birthday."

He finally meets my gaze and there's a softness

there that I hardly ever see from him, but it's the side I pine for most.

"I didn't think it was important," I try to speak, but my words are whispered. Of every reason I'm breaking apart, that fact is meaningless and even speaking it as if it could contribute to this pain is disrespectful to the tragedies that surround us.

He's gentle as he repositions me on the desk but doesn't pull my dress back down. It's bunched at my hips and that's what I'm thinking about when I hear the first cuff open and look up at the feel of metal grazing the skin on my wrists.

"Your other hand," Carter commands and I give it to him although I'm riddled with a slight fear.

"Carter?" His name comes out as a question as he handcuffs me to two metal loops on the side of his desk. Again, he repositions me, sliding my body down so I'm stretched on my belly across his desk.

"I don't have a gift for you at the moment," he says absently as he steps away from me, leaving the cool air to hit my ass which is still very much exposed to him. "But I'll have to find something nice for you."

The flicker instantly morphs into a thrumming with a slight fear of the unknown.

I try to turn around and look at him as he fiddles with something on the shelf. I don't see what he has but whatever it is, he has it in his hand.

"Carter, I'm sorry." My first instinct is to beg my way out of another punishment. My ass is still so sore. But even as the adrenaline spikes through me, I can't imagine he'd do it. That he'd punish me for not telling him it was my birthday. "Please," I whimper.

"Hush," he says, and his voice is calming as he lays a hand down on my lower back. His touch is an instant salve to my nerves. The rough pads of his thumbs rub soothing circles and that alone calms me. "This is for pleasure, songbird."

A slick oil drizzling between my ass crack makes me jump, but I'm held down by his hand and the cuffs. Again, he chuckles, deep and low at me, ever amused but I love it.

I love that sound.

"I need to spread you, and then you need to push back," he commands, and I force myself to swallow, feeling the pressure of a cool metal object press against my forbidden hole. I'm instantly hot and tense. The nerve endings come alive and the heat spreads like wildfire through my body and along my skin.

The thrumming intensifies, my heart slamming and lust consuming the ounce of fear that lingers.

A shudder of pleasure and a hint of stinging pain make me clench everything, but the second the tension is gone, Carter pushes the plug deeper inside of me. Oh. My. God.

I can barely breathe as the new sensation takes over. My nipples pebble and rub against the desk as I squirm beneath his ministrations. He fucks me with the butt plug, pushing it in and out, over and over.

"Carter," I moan and then whimper, feeling close to cumming so soon. I feel so full. So hot. The little hairs on the back of my neck rise as my head thrashes.

"Your cunt is clenching around nothing," Carter observes, and his deep voice forces my eyes open. Just as I feel the need to raise my ass higher, Carter pushes the plug in deeper and stops everything, leaving me feeling full and hot and on the edge of desire.

"Arch your back," Carter demands as he presses his fingers against my inner thigh, spreading my legs for him even though they tremble with the threat of an orgasm so close.

I swear I can feel it in my pussy. The arousal is there even though I'm so aware that nothing's inside of me... not there.

The metal of the cuffs digs into my skin, my ass is in the air, and each wrist bound to the desk. A soft moan escapes and the heated blushes rise up my face to my crown as Carter brushes his fingers across my clit and then up and down my pussy. "Should I tell your father the truth?" he asks me.

"Should I tell him I wanted you so badly that I was willing to start a war to keep you?"

While his words force a moan from me, they push my emotions over the edge.

It wasn't me he wanted.

The little voice in the back of my head reminds me, and I have to close my eyes tightly, pushing away the immediate sadness and dejection.

I feel tense and on edge in more ways than one. The swell of both emotion and lust beg me to tell him, but Carter's silent and his touch absent. I force my eyes open to see him watching me. His dark eyes staring deep into mine, searching for something.

I know I should tell him, but if he knew the girl who banged on the door calling out that she was in need wasn't me, would he want me still? I can't bear for that answer to be no.

"Do I need to gag you?" Carter asks. My heart hammers and my pulse quickens.

"For what?" I ask in return, but then immediately assure him, "I can be quiet," for whatever he's thinking. I'll do anything he asks.

"It's time to call your father," he tells me, and a mask slips over his face. An expression of indifference that makes the angular lines of his jaw look that much sharper. I can see the moment he changes into the Carter I first knew and hated. It happens right before my eyes; I see the darkness take over.

"You can stay on edge for it." His voice is a hum of both desire and amusement. "Think about how good it's going to feel when I fuck you and finally let you cum."

CHAPTER 24

Carter

ALL I CAN THINK ABOUT as the phone rings, is how much control I'm going to need not to fuck Aria senseless until she's screaming my name while her father is on the line.

I press the numbers slowly, one at a time, remembering the look of absolute agony on her face when I mentioned starting a war for her. I didn't mean for it to break her.

It's only the truth.

Putting the phone on speaker, the tension boils inside of me as the phone rings and Aria struggles on the desk.

Ring.

I trail my finger down her backside all the way to

her knee, and she whimpers. "Hush," I tell her, watching goosebumps form along her smooth skin.

Ring.

"You don't want your father to hear you," I say and don't bother to whisper. The sound of her breathing hitching begs me to look into her eyes. They're pleading with me, and I swear I'll try to give her something from this call.

Something that will help her.

I'll show her what kind of a man her father is.

Ring.

The third ring is only partial, followed by a low click and a pause before I hear the voice of my enemy. "Cross," he answers the phone.

Anger erupts up my throat at the sound of his voice. I can only concentrate on Aria's tempting body sprawled on my desk to calm me. Oh, and she does. Letting my fingers delight in her soft touch, I drag them up her wet lips and slowly push against the plug in her ass.

The suppressed moan tugs a sick smile onto my face as I answer, "Talvery."

Continuing to fuck her ass with the plug and reveling in the faint sounds of the metal clinking as Aria tries her damnedest to both hold still and quiet the sounds of pleasure gathering inside of her and threatening to go off at any moment, I speak clearly, "I thought you may want to have a conversation?"

There's silence on the other end as Aria's lips form a perfect O and her lower back and thighs tremble. She's so fucking close. Slipping a finger inside of her cunt, I use enough pressure to get her off.

"Maybe about my arrangements with your daughter?"

Her leg raises and slams down on the desk, twice. Two loud slams that jostle the phone as her face scrunches and she bites into her lip.

That's once.

"You son of a bitch," Talvery sneers at me, oblivious to what I've just done to his daughter.

Aria's eyes pop open, although her face is still flushed and she's struggling to breathe quietly.

"Don't you know you should have more respect for women than that?" I tell Talvery and drag my fingers back down to Aria's clit. The shiver that runs through her makes it all the more thrilling.

"How did you get her?" Talvery's question makes me pause, taking my fingers away from her to consider his question. His *first* question. Not whether or not she's well or safe, but *how* did I get her.

Two options exist. He knows of the informant and wants it verified, or he truly has no idea.

"She was a gift," I explain to him evenly, my eyes narrowing on the phone and waiting for his response to give me more insight.

The sound of Aria's sharp inhale reminds me of my songbird, and that she's listening. Leaning forward, I plant a kiss on her thigh, one meant to soothe whatever pained thoughts are running through her head.

"From Romano?" he asks me, breathing heavier into the phone. "Is that what you expect me to believe?" he sneers, and Aria raises her head on the desk, ready to object and speak up, but I silence her, gripping her chin and shaking my head once. I know my expression is hard as fucking stone, which is what makes her flinch, but she cannot be allowed to speak to him.

I won't let her be any more involved in this war than she already is.

"You can believe what you want. You asked a question. I answered."

She's tense on the desk and she's facing away from me, trying to look at the phone, as if there's anything there to see.

She scissors her legs, to turn her body so she can see the phone, and again my lips tug into a smile when she moans softly.

He can't hear her as he tells me, "I've been informed."

I don't give him much thought. I know what he's been told, and he can go fuck himself with that misinformation, while I fuck his daughter.

I move back to her ass, teasing her and fucking her with the plug. Her nails scratch against the table as she tries to fight the desire to moan out loud.

I hit mute for just a moment, ready to hear that sweet sound I love. Her father continues although he can't hear us in return.

"What'd you do to her?"

I whisper to Aria, grabbing her ass with my other hand and forcing that beautiful sound to spill from her lips. The mix of intense pleasure and sting of pain too much for her to control. "Look at me while I fuck your ass, Aria." Her eyes widen with fear and I smirk as I explain, "He can't hear you, but I'm unmuting now, so be quiet, songbird."

Those beautiful lips part with both a sigh of relief and then a quiet whimper of pleasure as I go back to teasing her pretty little cunt. Her eyes nearly close, but she whips them open, obeying my last command to look at me.

"I'll kill you if you touched her." Talvery issues a false threat as I unmute the conversation.

"How could I not touch her?" I ask him.

I hear a small whimper of protest from Aria and feel like a prick that I'm goading her father in front of her.

With apprehension coiling in the pit of my stomach, I speak. "I've given her everything she needs. She's having hard days." Although her father is listening, these words are just for her as I add, "She seems to be fitting in well, and at times she even seems happy."

Her hazel eyes soften and nearly gloss over, her eyes never faltering from my gaze.

"What do you want, Cross?" Talvery's harsh and bitter voice forces my jaw to clench.

I think about telling him how she told me she loves me. But repeating those words to him and using them like that would be a travesty.

She's calmer, wide-eyed and waiting with bated breath for my answer.

"Just to talk. I have someone here who wanted to hear your voice."

I push my fingers into her tight cunt and my thumb presses against the butt plug. The clinking of the handcuffs is loud enough for Talvery to hear and knowing that, a conceited grin stretches across my face.

"Let me speak to her," he says but his demand is pathetic. I'd never do anything because he ordered it. I'd go through hell just to spite him.

"She's a little tied up at the moment," I tell him, feeling the arrogance surge inside of me, but wanting to contain it enough to keep it from hurting my Aria. I circle her clit ruthlessly, knowing she gets off so easily with this touch. I'd rather she be in such blinding pleasure that she can't hear or even comprehend the conversation.

"I'll fucking kill you," he says, and he doesn't hide the anger in his voice.

"You keep trying to do that," I retort and the anger seeps into my voice with every passing moment. And although concern is clearly written on Aria's expression, her thighs tremble with the upcoming release and her teeth sink into her bottom lip so hard she'll be tasting blood if she bites any harder.

I mute the conversation again for only a second to command her, "Cum for me, Aria." And then finger fuck her harder.

Her back bows and a soft, strangled cry slips by her lips just as I tell Talvery, "I promise I'm being good to her. I know how to treat a woman."

At my words, she cums, hard and violently. Her entire body showing the tremors of pleasure that race through her.

"Did Romano tell you what she did?" I ask Talvery,

more to remind myself. This strong woman is mine. I'm fucking proud to have her as mine.

"Stephan?" Talvery asks as Aria's eyes meet mine and I whisper harshly in response, irritated by his interruption, "Yes."

Breathing heavily, Aria tries to look up; she tries to will the phone to give her more of a response from her father.

But nothing comes.

There's nothing but silence on the other line.

And I hate him for it. Truly hate him for the tears he brings to her eyes.

"You didn't come for her." I have to swallow the spiked ball growing in my throat. "How long have you known?"

When he doesn't reply, the edge of hate comes on thicker and I say, "I know Romano spilling a little secret wasn't what tipped you off."

Her face crumples and I lean forward, kissing every inch of the curve of her waist.

"Give her a message for me," Talvery says, but I ignore him in preference for the sweet sounds of gratitude I can barely hear from Aria.

"I couldn't tell her before this, but I'm telling her right now."

"I'm listening," I tell him, only to mute the phone again as I kiss Aria's reddened skin on her ass and gently move the butt plug in and out once again. She's so close already.

"Tell her I said, 'Stay quiet while I'm gone and stay in her room.'"

Unmuting the phone, I answer him quickly, "I'll be sure to let her know," and then hang up the phone, done with him and this conversation. And ready to hear her scream my name.

Moving her legs off the desk and fueled by her gasp and the sounds of her nails scratching along the desk, I unleash my cock and shove myself all the way in her to the hilt.

"Fuck, yes," I groan as my limbs tingle. "Fuck, I need you," I whisper along her back as I lower my lips to kiss along her skin. I stay still inside of her, letting her adjust and waiting to make sure she feels nothing but pleasure.

"You have no idea how much I want him to know you scream my name every night."

"Is he—" Aria asks before throwing her head back with a strangled cry of pleasure as I slam inside of her again.

Still, she turns to look at the phone, with her face scrunched and struggling to stay quiet, and I know she's wondering if he can hear.

Even as my cock is inside of her heat, she worries.

I won't fucking allow it.

I bang the phone down over and over, so she can hear. One hand on the phone, the other with a bruising grip on her hip. I fuck her in time with the violent banging until she can register the dead tone.

Shoving the phone off the desk, I tell her, "He doesn't matter. Nothing else matters." My words come out with a hard grunt as her pussy spasms around my thick length. "There's only us," I push the words out, pistoning my hips and feeling my balls draw up once again.

As I pound into her, I ask her, "How does it feel to have your ass and pussy filled at the same time?"

"Carter," she whimpers my name as she cums again. And then again. As I ride through her pleasure, each one harder and stronger than the last, I beg my body not to give in.

I want to stay in this moment forever. Her chained to my desk, feeling nothing but the heat of my desire and the thrill of me fucking her until her legs are weak and shaking.

But I have to. And on the third time her cunt grips my dick with her orgasm, I thrust myself as deep inside of her as I can, and cum harder than I ever have in my life.

I'm breathless when I pull the plug from her, giving her yet another wave of pleasure. I'm panting when I uncuff her and pull her into my lap to feel her heated skin tremble against mine.

The sound of our mingled breathing doesn't last long. Aria's hair tickles along my shoulder as she pulls away from me, reaching for the phone.

Her shoulders shake with her ragged breath and her eyes look lost in the distance.

"It's fine," I tell her, the swell of rage and worse, disappointment, brewing inside of me.

"Can I call him back?" Her question is immediate and laced with a mix of fear and worry. "Just me, please?" she begs me in a broken whisper.

Watching her swallow, I gauge her desperation that seemingly came from nowhere.

"I don't trust your father," I tell her honestly.

"You can trust me," she suggests weakly, the pleading tone still present.

I give her silence as I search her gaze and the desperation transforms to anger when she adds, "You didn't have to taunt him like that," but her voice cracks.

She's worried. Something's wrong

"Please let me call him back," she begs again. "I promise it's okay. I just want to tell him I'm all right." She worries her bottom lip between her teeth as she looks me in the eyes, both of her hands gripping on to me.

"No, what's wrong?" She won't look me in the eye at my response, so I grab her chin, forcing her eyes up and searching for the truth inside of them.

"WHY DOES it have to be like this?" Her words crack, and tears leak from the corners of her eyes.

"What the hell happened?" My eyes narrow as I watch her lose it. Losing every ounce of composure. "What's wrong?"

"I love you," she answers with pain. "I'm sorry," she whimpers, wiping her eyes and trying to get away from me and out of my hold.

"I would never hurt you," I tell her as my heart races, knowing I can't give her the same words back. "You know that?" Going over everything that happened, all I can think is that it's the way I spoke about how she came to me. The way we started and the arrogance I showed. "The way I was talking-"

She stops me, pressing her fingers to my lips, "I would never hurt you either."

My phone going off distracts me; the message is from Jase. *You need to see this, now.*

Pressing a kiss to her soft lips, I try to end her worries. She attempts to deepen it, but I pull away, pressing my forehead to hers and wishing I didn't have to leave her right now.

I whisper against her lips, "Wait for me in the bedroom." I open my eyes to see the longing in hers and a well of emotion that knows no depths.

She only nods, loosening her grip as I set her down on the ground and stand up with her.

"I have something to take care of and then I'll come to you," I tell her, but her expression is absent of accepting a thing I'm telling her. One day she'll understand that I'll take care of everything so long as she trusts me to.

But she goes just the same and I watch her walk away from me as I stand outside the office door, wondering if she holds the same opinion of her father now that she did hours ago.

She glances behind her one last time, giving me a sad smile before disappearing around the corner to the stairwell.

I DON'T MAKE it down the hall before Jase is up the

stairs, full steam in his gait until he lifts his head and sees me.

"We need to talk." Jase's voice carries down the hall with an edge of urgency. "Now."

"What's going on?" I ask him, feeling my forehead crease and the adrenaline pumping harder.

"There's been a breach. Looks like we're going to have company." His eyes reflect the welcome of a challenge and my lips curl up in agreement.

"Talvery?" I ask him, wondering if her father was already in motion before the call, or if he stupidly acted off impulse.

Jase nods, but worry lines his expression. "There are only six."

"Six men?" I question. "Talvery isn't that fucking stupid."

"One's an informant and probably how they got past the first gate. Two are her blood."

"You think someone helped him?" I question Jase, thinking the informant was aided by someone he's spoken to, but he shakes his head quickly.

"We were alerted the second they were spotted. Where's Aria?" Jase questions and I'm quick to answer, "She's safe in my bedroom. She won't leave."

My throat dries and tightens, thinking about them stealing her, but worry and fear will only bring my downfall.

"There's no way he thought he could succeed in doing anything but sending his own men to be killed with only six."

"There's definitely something off," he adds and pulls

up the feed on his phone. Six men along the inner tower, fully armored. I watch with him as he asks me, "We could question them?"

My chest tightens as I recognize the face of one man. "Nikolai."

He dared to come here. To try to take what's mine? Anger fills my blood and a seething mix of jealousy and vengeance turns my vision red.

"I was thinking we eliminate the three that don't matter but bring the cousins and Nikolai in for questioning." His statement is spoken in a low voice as he looks behind us, back to where Aria waits for me.

I lick my lips, knowing that Talvery is fully aware all six would die in an attempt to infiltrate and kill us, to rescue Aria.

"Nikolai is foolish and desperate. If he came because he knew she was here, I could see him only being followed by a few men."

"They're all high ranking," I say quickly, knowing each one of them. Recognizing a few who have killed on my streets.

"There's no way they came without Talvery knowing."

"Did they come to kill? Or to take her?" I ask Jase but had I waited for a second longer, I wouldn't have had to ask at all. I watch as one of them drops a grenade on the edge of the garage, followed by another a few feet farther down. *They came to kill.*

"They left explosives lining the gate. A scan shows they have enough on the bags strapped to their backs for the entire estate if they could get through it." My lips twitch with menace. "The same as before?" I ask Jase, remembering the site of the ash and rubble my former home was made to be. "You think it's the same men?"

Jase and I share a look, but he doesn't answer me verbally.

A call to Jase's phone replaces the surveillance on his phone. The moment he answers, my own phone rings to life in my pocket.

"It's Aria," Jase tells me before I answer my phone. He doesn't hide the nervousness as he tells me, "She's not staying in the bedroom."

"Where is she going?" I ask him, but then realize it doesn't matter. If she sees, she'll have to choose.

"Let her be, let her come if she chooses." My heart races as Jase tells them my orders and my phone dies in my hand. She'll see what they're capable of and what I need to stop, what I need to protect.

Let her see, let her choose.

"Have them kill the three, now." My voice is hard although inside tremors of rage grow. The three bodies will drop the second the command is given, leaving the other three scrambling but trapped on our estate. "Bring the other three to me."

CHAPTER 25

Aria

I**F ONLY** C**ARTER** would let me call my father or go to him. My skin pricks with goosebumps that won't leave and the constant chill I feel is at odds with the heat boiling my blood.

I can convince my father that there's another way.

I heard what he said. The message for me. He was speaking in code. He's coming. In only hours, my father is coming for me.

Stay quiet while I'm gone and stay in your room.

My father would tell me that before leaving for the night when we were on lockdown, but only when he would be gone for a few hours. If it was any longer than that, he'd have me go to the safe house.

There's no way those words were a coincidence. I'm

sure of it. He wouldn't have said it if he wasn't coming for me. He wouldn't have said *those words* if something wasn't happening by tonight.

My heart hasn't stopped racing. My throat is tight with guilt and fear. It can't happen like this. I don't know exactly what he's planning, but those are words said in times of war. Something bad is going to happen. I know it. I can feel it in the pit of my stomach. It's going to change everything.

I can do something. But I need time that I don't have.

Pacing up and down the corridor to Carter's wing in the estate, I try to formulate an excuse for my father or a reason that would justify Carter not reacting to my father's threats. I can't go into the bedroom and just wait. I refuse to simply stand by.

The conversation that was just had on the phone repeats itself over and over again in my head and I start to debate if I heard my father right.

Tension squeezes my chest so tightly I can't breathe.

After days, my father decides to come. After weeks of me being missing, he's finally coming for me. And there's nothing I can do to stop him.

My hands are shaking horribly, and it does nothing but piss me off. Forming a fist, I slam it into the wall. How could he do this to me?

Both of them.

Carter's not innocent. He knew that conversation would piss my father off. He was goading him, practically laughing in my father's face.

And I took pleasure in it.

Every bit of that pleasure I wanted. There's something sick and twisted about how I craved Carter pushing me to the edge while my father spat hate at him.

Carter has proven there's a side to me that desires depravity and a sense of justice that's sinful and warped.

I should have known better. We were playing with fire but after weeks of being with Carter, of being his, of growing to love him made me feel invincible beside him.

I've always been foolish like that.

Brushing the hair away from my face, I rid myself of the regret and focus on the now and the present.

I have to tell Carter, but I don't know how I can save my father if I do. And I know it won't be my father coming. He won't storm Carter's castle. It'll be hired men, or worse, Nikolai. Telling Carter will only ensure that his guns will be ready and whoever is coming will be killed before they even come close.

"Fuck." The word slips from my lips in a strangled breath.

I was so full of hope, so eager to have this call happen, and instead, my worst nightmare has come to life. I've brought the war to me and to Carter's doorstep.

A moment of clarity comes over me, and my eyes whip open.

I start moving before the thought is even clear.

He's not in the office. Carter is not in the office

where the phone is. *And I don't remember him locking the door.*

I'm well aware that Carter has cameras everywhere, and that's why I walk as if nothing's wrong. My shoulders are square, and I try to keep my expression impassive even though tears prick at my eyes and my chest hiccups with the need to break down.

These men will kill me before they get a chance to kill each other.

The doorknob rattles under my grip, but it turns, and the door pushes open easily. I don't waste any time, knowing Carter will come if he sees me, and I fall to my knees, gathering the phone still carelessly tossed on the floor from earlier.

My finger shakes as I press the buttons, but I do it. I grip the phone with both hands as I hold it to my ear and watch the door. If he doesn't know already, he'll know soon enough.

Ring, ring.

Every pause of the ring grips my heart harder.

My throat feels as if it's closed up, clogged by something unseen when the call goes dead. Not unanswered, but dead.

Clank! I slam the phone down over and over again, just as Carter did before, feeling the heat of anxiety roll over my skin. My teeth are clenched as I slam it down again before bracing myself over the desk.

Deep breaths. I need to stay calm and find a way.

Not another second passes. Not another tense breath heaves from me before I pick up the phone and hit redial again.

To no avail.

Tick-tock, tick-tock, the clock on Carter's office wall taunts me. Showing nearly fifty minutes have passed since Carter left me.

The only other number I know by heart is Nikolai's. I don't know if he would listen. Or if my father would listen to Nikolai. I don't know anything for certain, but still, I dial in his number.

One number at a time.

And he doesn't answer.

The phone goes to voicemail, but the inbox is full. A ball of barbed wire seems to unwind in my throat as hopelessness steals the breath from me. With every breath, I swallow more of it and it pains my chest. My fingers dig into my shirt right over my heart, gripping and trying to pull the spiked pain away. But it only grows.

Tick-tock. Tick-tock.

I try my father's number again, putting it on speaker this time, giving up any pretense I had before. If Carter walks in, I'll tell him everything. There's not any other light of hope left in the dark clouds that settle around me.

With the sound of the dead tone coming from the phone, I set the phone down, politely resting it in its cradle, and collapse into Carter's seat.

I try Carter's computer. It's password protected.

I type in Tyler. Rejected.

Cross. Rejected. I would try birthdays and old exes if I knew any. But I don't have a damn thing to work with.

My mind wars with itself, the stakes growing higher and higher as the seconds pass. Pulling open his drawer and flipping through files I try to find anything that could hint at his password, but I come up with nothing.

Tick-tock. Tick-tock.

The clock plays tricks on me. An hour and a half has passed.

My pulse is so fast; I can't hear anything else. I feel dizzy and lightheaded as I stand up and I have to brace myself to keep from falling over. The desk feels so cold and hard and the edges of it sharper than they did before.

I squeeze them so tightly that I think I may have cut myself but when I look down, there's been no blood shed.

"I have to tell him," I whisper to no one.

I can't balance myself as I walk. I have to rest my head against the wall for only a moment to catch my breath and think of the right words to say, the only words to say.

My father is coming. Men are coming to kill you.

I fight back the rush of oncoming tears and force myself to move. *Or maybe only to rescue me.*

I shut the door behind me and take in a shuddering breath.

I walk down the hall toward the stairwell, feeling cold and numb.

Deep breaths, one foot in front of the other. That's how I'll end my father's life and all those who stand with him. My cousins, my uncles. *Nikolai.*

God help me, please.

I pray as I grip the railing tightly and take each step carefully as my knees feel weaker.

Show me what to do. Please.

I'm halfway down the second set of stairs, toward the back half of the estate I never venture to, when I hear a gun cock. I freeze.

The sounds of a slap and a grunt mix with a cry of agony. My knees nearly buckle. *They're here.*

I'm too late. *No, please no.*

"Fuck you." I hear a voice I think belongs to one of my cousins and another hard smack as my knuckles go white from gripping the railing.

I can't breathe as my bare feet pad on the cold floor and I sneak closer to where the voices are coming from. My heart is beating so loud, I think they'll hear me.

How could I have let this happen?

How could Carter? The thought goes unfinished, but either way, my heart breaks.

"We'll take it from here," I hear Carter's voice as I see the backs of two men leaving, walking out from an open doorway, and heading to the rear exit. Both dressed in black and carrying guns. Not handguns or pistols, but automatic weapons. I nearly fall backward on my ass trying to take cover in the closest doorway, so I go unseen.

The sound of metal scraping against the floor can only be guns being kicked away.

Guns and questioning. It's an interrogation. My heart races and I struggle with what I can do to stop this.

"Where is she?"

Nikolai. I grip the wall, just around the corner from the front room where the voices carry from. The mix of adrenaline, fear, and betrayal riding through my veins in waves and overwhelming my ability to even think.

"I'll ask again, nicely. What were your direct orders?" Jase's voice is cold. Colder and harsher than I ever could have imagined. "Or did you not have any?"

I can barely breathe and when I do, it sounds so loud. My heart's beating out of my chest when I peek around the corner, getting low to the ground and praying no one will see me.

"Did your boss really send you to your death on a whim? Six men against an army?"

I cover my mouth with both of my hands and nearly fall forward at the sight in front of me as I round the corner, the rushing of my blood drowns out the voices of the interrogation, but the sound of a gun smacking against skin and crashing into bone rings clearly.

With my eyes shut tightly and a sickness stirring in my stomach, I force my eyes open. I force myself to see everything.

Nikolai makes up one of the three. The other two are my cousins, Brett and Henry. They're brothers and years older than me. We've shared every holiday. I was a bridesmaid in Brett's wedding. Every event we've been to together for years flashes before my eyes as I see Brett spit blood onto the floor. The left side of his face is already bruised and the black chestplate of his armor is covered in blood.

My heart squeezes. I don't want to see this. I can't. I can't watch, but I have to do something.

"We're not telling you shit," Brett sneers and Henry struggles next to him. With their wrists bound behind their backs, Henry sways. His right eye is swollen and that's all I can see, but he's not well.

What did they do to you? My heart bleeds at the question.

Jase and Declan have guns pointed at the back of their heads, with all three of them kneeling in a row in front of them.

"You want to join your friends sooner, rather than later?" Jase questions them.

I've never felt so betrayed. So sickened. Bile rises in my throat as my gaze drifts across the three men I've known all my life so close to their lives being over if only a trigger is pulled.

"Fuck you," Nikolai grunts out, pulling my focus to him. Although he stares at Carter with nothing but hate, his eyes show his pain. And it's my undoing.

The war has never felt so alive as it does now.

That's when I see a light shine, directing my eyes to what matters.

Carter's gun is tucked in the back of his pants. It's staring right at me, the light from the room reflecting on it. And the guns on the floor behind him. Three guns and one I recognize as Nikolai's.

He took their guns, he kicked them away from my family. And now they kneel in front of Jase and Declan, waiting for execution. The sound of a gun being cocked pushes me forward and leaves me no choice.

My hands shake as I crawl toward the guns. One scratches across the floor as I try to pick it up and I know at that point they see me. So, I do the only thing I can.

I point the gun at the enemy who doesn't have a gun.

I stand on weak legs and grip the gun as tightly as I can. Aiming it at the back of Carter's head. Knowing I've made a choice and hating myself for it but fueled by the need to protect my only friend and family.

"Carter," I call out his name and feel the eyes of everyone else in the room on me as Carter turns slowly around to face me.

His eyes flash as he lets out a breath, but he doesn't retreat, he doesn't even seem to take me seriously. He looks at me the way you'd look at a child playing dress-up. Non-threatening and as if they're simply being cute. It cuts me in a way I didn't think was possible.

He really cares so little for me. He's really going to kill them all and expects me to fall in line, obeying and submitting to his every whim.

As he steps toward me and I pull the trigger back even though my hands tremble, his expression morphs, and the damage I've done is so clear to me in this moment. His firm expression of disapproval and irritation changes to one I've never seen. A mask of hardness and sharpness that makes his chiseled features look even more dominating and villainous.

I can hear him breathe as he stops in his tracks.

Everything about him is terrifying, save the look in his eyes. Those dark eyes with bright specks of silver still shine with something else. Hope, maybe? But it vanishes when I call out to him, feeling the tightness in my throat and chest squeezing the courage from me. "Let them go," I force the words out and they come out strong. I don't know how because at the moment I feel nothing but weak.

I feel like I failed the boy still hurting inside of Carter. I've lost the trust. I can see it as Carter's eyes glaze over and the darkness overwhelms them. I've never hurt so much in my life as I do now, but what else was there for me to do? I'm in a hopeless situation and there's no possible way for me to win.

My palms are so hot and tingling with the rush of adrenaline and mix of fear that controls my every move, and I nearly drop the gun but somehow, I hold it steady and keep it pointed on Carter.

"The girl we've all been waiting for," Carter says without a change in his expression. No arrogant smile. Nothing but a menacing look of hatred and disgust.

His head tilts and he says a word low and deep in his throat that sends a sickening chill down my spine. "Talvery."

TO BE CONTINUED…

CARTER AND ARIA'S story continues in BREATHLESS!!

You don't want to miss what happens next in this gripping story!

HAVEN'T READ Daniel and Addison's story? You don't want to miss out on their heart-wrenching story, Possessive. Keep reading for a sneak peek.

KEEP READING at the very end for a preview of my *USA Today* Bestseller, Forget Me Not.

W WINTERS REAL

Sinful Obsessions Series:
It's Our Secret
Little Liar
Possessive
Merciless

Standalone Novels:
Broken
Forget Me Not

Sins and Secrets Duets:
Imperfect (Imperfect Duet book 1)
Unforgiven (Imperfect Duet book 2)

Damaged (Damaged Duet book 1)
Scarred (Damaged Duet book 2)

Happy reading and best wishes,
W Winters xx

SNEAK PEEK OF
POSSESSIVE

From *USA Today* bestselling author W Winters comes an emotionally gripping, standalone, contemporary romance.

It was never love with Daniel and I never thought it would be.

It was only lust from a distance.

Unrequited love maybe.

He's a man I could never have, for so many reasons.

That didn't stop my heart from beating wildly when his eyes pierced through me.

It only slowed back down when he'd look away,

making me feel so damn unworthy and reminding me that he would never be mine.

Years have passed and one look at him brings it all back.

But time changes everything.

There's a heat in his eyes I recognize from so long ago, a tension between us I thought was one-sided.

"Tell me you want it." His rough voice cuts through the night and I can't resist.

That's where my story really begins.

Possessive is an emotional, gripping story. Filled with heartache, guilt and longing! Possessive will take you on a journey of obsession and jealousy...it's emotional, raw and captivating. - **Beyond The Covers Blog**

PREFACE

Addison

*I*t's easy to smile around Tyler.

It's how he got me. We were in tenth-grade calculus, and he made some stupid joke about angles. I don't even remember what it was. Something about never discussing infinity with a mathematician because you'll never hear the end of it. He's a cute dork with his jokes. He knows some dirty ones too.

A year later and he still makes me smile. Even when we're fighting. He says he just wants to see me smile. How could I leave when I believe him with everything in me?

My friend's grandmother told me once to fall in love with someone who loves you just a little more.

Even as my shoulders shake with a small laugh and he leans forward nipping my neck, I know that I'll never really love Tyler the way he loves me.

And it makes me ashamed. Truly.

I'm still laughing when the bedroom door creaks open. Tyler plants a small kiss on my shoulder. It's not an open-mouth kiss, but still, it leaves a trace on my skin and sends a warmth through my body. It's only momentary though.

The cool air passes between the two of us, as Tyler leans back and smiles broadly at his brother.

I may be seated on my boyfriend's lap, but the way Daniel looks at me makes me feel alone. His eyes pierce through me. With a sharpness that makes me afraid to move. Afraid to breathe even.

I don't know why he does this to me.

He makes me hot and cold at the same time. It's like I've disappointed him simply by being here. As if he doesn't like me. Yet, there's something else.

Something that's forbidden.

It creeps up on me whenever I hear Daniel's rough voice; whenever I catch him watching Tyler and me. It's like I've been caught cheating, which makes no sense at all. I don't belong to Daniel, no matter how much that idea haunts my dreams.

He's almost twenty and I'm only sixteen. And more importantly, he's Tyler's brother.

It's all in my head. I tell myself over and over again that the electricity between us is something I've made up. That my body doesn't burn for Daniel. That my soul doesn't ache for him to rip me away and punish me for daring to let his brother touch me.

It's only when Tyler says something to him, that Daniel turns to look at him, tossing something down beside us.

Tyler's oblivious to everything happening. And suddenly, I can breathe again.

My eyelids flutter open, my body hot under the stifling blankets. I don't react to the memory in my dreams anymore. Not at first. It sinks in slowly. The recognition of what that day would lead to getting heavier in my heart with each second that passes. Like a wave crashing on the shore, but it's taking its time. Threatening as it approaches.

It was years ago, but the memory stays.

The feeling of betrayal, for fantasizing about Tyler's older brother.

The heartache from knowing what happened only three weeks after that night.

The desire and desperation to go back to that point and beg Tyler to never come looking for me.

All of those needs stir into a deadly concoction in the pit of my stomach. It's been years since I've been tormented by the memories of Tyler and what we had. And by the memories of Daniel and what never was.

Years have passed.

But it all comes back now that Daniel's back.

CHAPTER 1

Addison
The night before

I LOVE THIS BAR. Iron Heart Brewery. It's nestled in the center of the city and located at the corner of this street. The town itself has history. Hints of the old cobblestone streets peek through the torn asphalt and all the signs here are worn and faded, decorated with weathered paint. I can't help but to be drawn here.

And with the varied memorabilia lining the walls, from signed knickknacks to old glass bottles of liquor, this place is flooded with a welcoming warmth. It's a quiet bar with all local and draft beers a few blocks away from the chaos of campus. So it's just right for me.

"Make up your mind?"

My body jolts at the sudden question. It only gets me a rough laugh from the tall man on my left, the bartender who spooked me. A grey shirt with the brewery logo on it fits the man well, forming to his muscular shoulders. With a bit of stubble and a charming smirk, he's not bad looking. And at that thought, my cheeks heat with a blush.

I could see us making out behind the bar; I can even hear the bottles clinking as we crash against the wall in a moment of passion. But that's where it would end for me. No hot and dirty sex on the hard floor. No taking him back to my barely furnished apartment.

I roll my eyes at the thought and blow a strand of hair away from my face as I meet his gaze.

I'm sure he flirts with everyone. But it doesn't make it any less fun for the moment.

"Whatever your favorite is," I tell him sheepishly. "I'm not picky." I have to press my lips together and hold back my smile when he widens his and nods.

"You new to town?" he asks me.

I shrug and have to slide the strap to my tank top back up onto my shoulder. Before I can answer, the door to the brewery and bar swings open, bringing in the sounds of the nightlife with it. It closes after two more customers leave. Looking over my shoulder through the large glass door at the front, I can see them heading out. The woman is leaning heavily against a strong man who's obviously her significant other.

Giving the bartender my attention again, I'm very much aware that there are only six of us here now. Two older men at the high top bar, talking in hushed voices and occasionally laughing so loud that I have to take a peek at them.

And one other couple who are seated at a table in the corner of the bar. The couple who just left had been sitting with them. All four are older than I am. I'd guess married with children and having a night out on the town.

And then there's the bartender and me.

"I'm not really from here, no."

"Just passing through?" he asks me as he walks toward the bar. I'm a table away, but he keeps his eyes on me as he reaches for a glass and hits the tap to fill it with something dark and decadent.

"I'm thinking about going to the university actually. To study business. I came to check it out." I don't tell him that I'm putting down some temporary roots regardless of whether or not I like the school here. Every year or so I move somewhere new ... searching for what could feel like home.

His eyebrow raises and he looks me up and down, making me feel naked. "Your ID isn't fake, right?" he asks and then tilts the tall glass in his hand to let the foam slide down the side.

"It isn't fake, I swear," I say with a smile and hold up my hands in defense. "I chose to travel instead of going to college. I've got a little business, but I thought finally learning more about the technicalities of it all would be a step in the right direction." I pause, thinking about how a degree feels more like a distraction than anything else. It's a reason to settle down and stop moving from place to place. It could be the change I need. Something needs to change.

His expression turns curious and I can practically hear all the questions on his lips. *Where did you go? What did you do? Why did you leave your home so young and naïve?* I've heard them all before and I have a prepared list of answers in my head for such questions.

But they're all lies. Pretty little lies.

He cleans off the glass before walking back over and pulling out the seat across from me.

Just as the legs of the chair scrape across the floor, the door behind me opens again, interrupting our conversation and the soft strums of the acoustic guitar playing in the background.

The motion brings a cold breeze with it that sends goosebumps down my shoulder and spine. A chill I can't ignore.

The bartender's ass doesn't even touch the chair. Whoever it is has his full attention.

As I lean down to reach for the cardigan laying on top of my purse, he puts up a finger and mouths, "One second."

The smile on my face is for him, but it falters when I hear the voice behind me.

Everything goes quiet as the door shuts and I listen to them talking. My body tenses and my breath leaves me. Frozen in place, I can't even slip on the cardigan as my blood runs cold.

My heart skips one beat and then another as a rough laugh rises above the background noise of the small bar.

"Yeah, I'll take an ale, something local," I hear Daniel say before he slips into view. I know it's him. That voice haunted me for years. His strides are confident and strong, just like I remember them. And as he passes me to take a seat by the bar, I can't take my eyes off of him.

He's taller and he looks older, but the slight resemblance to Tyler is still there. As my heart learns its rhythm again, I notice his sharp cheekbones and my gaze drifts to his hard jaw, covered with a five o'clock shadow. I'd always thought of him as tall and handsome, albeit in a dark and brooding way. And that's still true.

He could fool you with his charm, but there's a darkness that never leaves his eyes.

His fingers spear through his hair as he checks out the beer options written in chalk on the board behind the bar. His hair's longer on top than it is on the sides, and I can't help but to imagine what it would feel like to grab on to it. It's a fantasy I've always had.

The timbre in his voice makes my body shudder.

And then heat.

I watch his throat as he talks, I notice the little movements as he pulls out a chair in the corner of the bar across from me. If only he would look my way, he'd see me.

Breathe. Just breathe.

My tongue darts out to lick my lips and I try to avert my eyes, but I can't.

I can't do a damn thing but wait for him to notice me.

I almost whisper the command, *look at me*. I think it so loud I'm sure it can be heard by every soul in this bar.

And finally, as if hearing the silent plea, he looks my way. His knuckles rap the table as he waits for his beer, but they stop mid-motion when his gaze reaches mine.

There's a heat, a spark of recognition. So intense and so raw that my body lights, every nerve ending alive with awareness.

And then it vanishes. Replaced with a bitter chill as he turns away. Casually. As if there was nothing there. As if he doesn't even recognize me.

I used to think it was all in my mind back then. Five years ago when we'd share a glance and that same feeling would ignite within me.

But this just happened. I know it did.

And I know he knows who I am.

With anger beginning to rise, my lips part to say his name, but it's caught in my throat. It smothers the sadness that's rising just as quickly. Slowly my fingers curl, forming a fist until my nails dig into my skin.

I don't stop staring at him, willing him to look at me and at least give me the courtesy of acknowledging me.

I know he can feel my eyes on him. He's stopped rapping his knuckles on the table and the smile on his face has faded.

Maybe the crushing feeling in my chest is shared by both of us.

Maybe I'm only a reminder to him. A reminder he ran away from too.

I don't know what I expected. I've dreamed of running into Daniel so many nights. Brushing shoulders on the way into a coffee shop. Meeting each other again through new friends. Every time I wound up back home, if you can even call it that, I always checked out every person passing me by, secretly wishing one would be him. Just so I'd have a reason to say his name.

Winding up at the same bar on a lonely Tuesday night hours away from the town we grew up in ... that was one of those daydreams too. But it didn't go like this in my head.

"Daniel." I say his name before I can stop myself. It comes out like a croak and he reluctantly turns his head as the bartender sets down the beer on the wooden table.

I swear it's so quiet, I can hear the foam fizzing as it settles in the glass.

His lips part just slightly, as if he's about to speak. And then he visibly inhales. It's a sharp breath and matches the gaze he gives me. First it's one of confusion, then anger ... and then nothing.

I have to remind my lungs to do their job as I clear my throat to correct myself, but both efforts are in vain.

He looks past me as if it wasn't me who was trying to get his attention.

"Jake," he speaks up, licking his lips and stretching his back. "I actually can't stay," he bellows from his spot to where the bartender, apparently named Jake, is chucking ice into a large glass. The music seems to get louder as the crushing weight of being so obviously dismissed and rejected settles in me.

I'm struck by how cold he is as he gets up. I can't stand to look at him as he readies to leave, but his name leaves me again. This time with bite.

His back stiffens as he shrugs his thin jacket around his shoulders and slowly turns to look at me.

I can feel his eyes on me, commanding me to look back at him and I do. I dare to look him in the eyes and say, "It's good to see you." It's surprising how even the words come out. How I can appear to be so calm when inside I'm burning with both anger and … something else I don't care to admit. What a lie those words are.

I hate how he gets to me. How I never had a choice.

With a hint of a nod, Daniel barely acknowledges me. His smile is tight, practically nonexistent, and then he's gone.

Possessive is Available Now!

SNEAK PEEK OF FORGET ME NOT

I fell in love with a boy a long time ago.

I was only a small girl. Scared and frightened, I was taken from my home and held against my will. His father hurt me, but he protected me and kept me safe as best he could.

Until I left him.

I ran the first chance I got and even though I knew he wasn't behind me, I didn't stop. The branches lashed out at me, punishing me for leaving him in the hands of a monster.

I've never felt such guilt in my life.

Although I survived, the boy was never found. I prayed for him to be safe. I dreamed he'd be alright and come back to me. Even as a young girl I knew I loved him, but I betrayed him.

Twenty years later, all my wishes came true.

But the boy came back a man. With a grip strong enough to keep me close and a look in his eyes that warned me to never dare leave him again. I was his to keep after all.

Twenty years after leaving one hell, I entered another. Our tale was only just getting started.

It's dark and twisted.

But that doesn't make it any less of what it is.

A love story. Our love story.

PROLOGUE

Robin

I can wait here longer than he can stand to stay away. I know that much.

A small grin pulls at my lips as I pick at the thread on the comforter. Always picking and waiting. There's nothing else to do in this room.

My head lifts at the thought, drawing my eyes to the blinking red light. And he's always watching. The sight of the camera makes my stomach churn, but only for a moment.

The sound of heavy boot steps walking down the stairs outside the closed door makes my heart race. I stare at the doorknob, willing it to turn and bring him to me.

I've waited too long for him.

The sound of the door opening is foreboding. If anyone other than me was waiting for him, I'd assume they'd have terror in their hearts. But I know him. I understand it all. The pain, the guilt. I know firsthand what it's like when the monster is gone and you only have your own thoughts to fight. Your memories and regrets. It's all-consuming.

And there's no one who can understand you. No one you trust, whose words you can believe are genuine and not just disguised pity.

But he knows me, and I know him. Far too well; our pain is shared.

His broad shoulders fill the doorway and his dark eyes meet mine instantly. He barely touches the door and it closes behind him with a loud click that's only a hair softer than my wildly beating heart.

It's hard to swallow, but I do. And I ignore the heat, the quickened breath. I push it all down as he walks toward me, closing the space with one heavy step at a time.

He stops in front of me, but doesn't hesitate to cup my chin in his large hand and I lean into his comforting touch. I know to keep my own hands down though and I grip the comforter instead of him.

It's a violent pain that rips through me, knowing how scarred he is. So much so, that I have to hold back everything. I'm afraid of my words, my touch. He's so close to being broken beyond repair and I only want to save him, but I don't know how.

We're both damaged, but the tortured soul in front of me makes me feel everything. He makes me want to live and heal his tormented soul. But how can I, when I'm the one who broke him by running away?

"My little bird," he whispers and it reminds me of when we were children. When we were trapped together.

He's not the boy who protected me.

He's not the boy whose eyes were filled with a darkness barely tempered with guilt.

He's not the boy I betrayed the moment I had a chance.

He's a man who's taking what he wants.

AND THAT'S ME.

CHAPTER 1

Robin
One week before

"Doctor Everly?" a soft voice calls out, breaking me from my distant thoughts as another early spring chill whips through my thin jacket and sends goosebumps down my body. I slowly turn my head to Karen. Her cheeks are a little too pink from a combination of the harsh wind and a heavy-handed application of blush, and the tip of her nose is a bright red.

I grip my thin jacket closer, huddling in it as if it can protect me from the brutal weather. It's too damn cold for spring, but I suppose I'd rather be cold and uncomfortable out here. Today especially.

I give Karen a tight smile, although I don't know why. It's not polite to smile out here, or is it? "How are you doing?" I ask her as she walks closer to me.

She nods her head, taking in a breath and looking past me at the pile of freshly upturned dirt. "It hurts still. It's just so sad." Karen's only twenty-three, fresh out of college and new to this. I'm new to it too. Marie was the first patient I've had who killed herself.

Sad isn't the right word for it. Devastating doesn't even begin to describe what it feels like when a young girl in your care decides her life is no longer worth living.

I clear my throat and turn on the grass to face her. The thin heels of my shoes sink into the soft ground, and I have to balance myself carefully just to stand upright.

"It is," I tell Karen, not sure what else to say.

"How do you handle..." her voice drifts off.

I don't know how to answer her. My lips part and I shake my head, but no words come out.

"I'm so sorry, Robin," she says and Karen's voice is strong and genuine. She knows how much Marie meant to me. But it wasn't enough.

I try to give her an appreciative smile, but I can't. Instead, I clear my tight throat and nod once, looking back to where Marie's buried.

"Are you okay?" she asks me cautiously, resting a hand on my arm, trying to comfort me. And I do what I shouldn't. *I lie.*

"I'm okay," I tell her softly, reaching up to squeeze her hand.

As I tuck a loose strand of hair behind my ear, a gust of wind flies by us and a bolt of lightning splits the sky into pieces, followed a few seconds later with the hard crack of thunder.

Karen looks up, and in an instant the light gray clouds darken and cue the storm to set in. It's only the two of us left here and it looks like the weather won't have us here any longer, leaving Marie all alone. I think deep inside that's how she wanted it all along. She didn't want a shrink to give her advice.

Who was I to help her? The guilt washes through me and the back of my eyes prick with unshed tears as I take in a shuddering breath, shoving my hands in my pockets and turning back to her grave.

As much as I'd like to believe I'll let her rest now, I know I'll be back. It's selfish of me. She just wanted to be left alone. She needed that so her past could fade into the background. I know that now; I wish I knew it then.

"She's in a better place," Karen whispers and my gaze whips up to hers. She doesn't have the decency to look me in the eyes and I have to wonder if she just said the words because she thinks they're appropriate. Like it's something meant to be said when talking of the dead, or maybe she really believes it.

Karen turns to walk toward her car as the sprinkling of rain starts to fall onto us. She looks back over her shoulder, waiting for me and I relent, joining her.

I'm sorry, Marie.

As the cold drops of rain turn to sheets and my hair dampens, my pace picks up. It doesn't take long until we're both jogging through the grass and then onto the pavement of the parking lot, our heels clicking and clacking on the pavement with the sound of the rain.

I barely hear her say goodbye and manage a wave behind me as I open my car door and sink into the driver seat.

I just wanted to help Marie. I could see so much of myself in her. We were almost the same age. She had the same look in her eyes. The same helplessness and lack of self-worth. I wanted to save her like my psychiatrist saved me.

But how could I? I'm not over my past. I should have known better. I should have referred her to someone more capable. Someone who had less emotional investment. I pushed too hard. *It's my fault.*

The pattering of rain on the car roof is eerily rhythmic as I dig through my purse, shivering and shoving the wet hair out of my face. The keys jingle as I shove them into the ignition, turning on the car and filling the cabin with the sounds of the radio.

I'm not sure what song's on but I don't care because I'm quick to turn the radio off. To get back to the silence and the peace of the rainfall. I slump in my seat, staring at the temperature gauge. When I look up, I see Karen drive away in the rearview mirror. Watching her car drive out of sight, my eyes travel to my reflection.

I scoff at myself and wipe under my eyes. I look dreadful. My dirty blonde hair's damp and disheveled, my makeup's running. I lift the console and grab a few tissues to clean myself up before sluggishly removing my soaked jacket and tossing it in the backseat. The heater finally kicks on, and I still can't bring myself to leave.

I look back into the mirror and see that I'm somewhat pulled together, but I can't hide the bags under my eyes. I can't force a false sense of contentment onto my face.

I close my eyes and take in another deep breath, filling my lungs and letting it out slowly. I need sleep. I need to eat. It's been almost a week since I found out about Marie. A week of her no longer being here to call and check in on. Tears stream freely down my cheeks. I tried so hard not to cry; I learned a long time ago that crying doesn't help, but being forced to leave her is making me helpless to my emotions.

That first night I almost cried, but instead I resorted to sleeping pills. A wave of nausea churns in my stomach at the thought of what I did. It was so easy to just take one after the other. Each one telling me it'd be over soon. After downing half the bottle, I knew what I was doing. But the entire bottle was too much and it all came back up before I could finish it. Thank God for that. I'm not well, and I'm sure as hell not in a position to help others.

My hand rests against my forehead as I try to calm down, as I try to rid myself of the vision of Marie in my office, but other memories of my past persist there, waiting for this weakness.

I can't linger any longer. Putting the car into reverse, I back out of my spot, turning and seeing Marie's plot in the distance as I back up.

Grief is a process, but guilt is something entirely

different. It's becoming harder and harder to separate the two, and I know why.

She reminds me of *him*.

Of a boy, I knew long ago. The turn signal seems louder than ever as I wait at the exit to turn onto the highway. *Click, click, click.*

Each is a second of time that I'm here and they're not. *Click, click, click.*

The cabin warms as I drive away, merging onto the highway.

Maybe all this has nothing to do with Marie.

Maybe it's just the guilt that summons the vision of his light gray eyes from the depths of my memory.

Maybe it's because I'm to blame for both of their deaths.

Forget Me Not is Available Now!

ABOUT W WINTERS

Thank you so much for reading my romances. I'm just a stay at home mom and avid reader turned author and I couldn't be happier.
I hope you love my books as much as I do!

More by W Winters
www.willowwinterswrites.com/books/